COUNTRY
LEGACY

COUNTRY
LEGACY

THE TEXAN'S
SURPRISE SON

NEW YORK TIMES BESTSELLING AUTHOR

Cathy McDavid

HARLEQUIN

Special thanks and acknowledgment are given
to Cathy McDavid for her contribution to
the Texas Rodeo Barons continuity.

Recycling programs
for this product may
not exist in your area.

ISBN-13: 978-1-335-52336-5

The Texan's Surprise Son
First published in 2014. This edition published in 2022.
Copyright © by Harlequin Enterprises ULC

For questions and comments about the quality of this book,
please contact us at CustomerService@Harlequin.com.

Harlequin Enterprises ULC
22 Adelaide St. West, 41st Floor
Toronto, Ontario M5H 4E3, Canada
www.Harlequin.com

Printed in U.S.A.

Since 2006, *New York Times* bestselling author **Cathy McDavid** has been happily penning contemporary Westerns for Harlequin. Every day, she gets to write about handsome cowboys riding the range or busting a bronc. It's a tough job, but she's willing to make the sacrifice. Cathy shares her Arizona home with her own real-life sweetheart and a trio of odd pets. Her grown twins have left to embark on lives of their own, and she couldn't be prouder of their accomplishments.

To my son, Clay.
I couldn't be more proud or more impressed
by the strides you've made in recent months.
This journey you're on is a difficult one,
but I'm with you every step of the way.

Love always,

Mom

Chapter 1

Only a fool would venture near eighteen hundred pounds of bucking bull crammed into a metal chute the size of a closet. Jacob Burke Baron not only went near the bull, he intended to ride the son of a gun. All the way to a win.

Eight seconds and a score better than eighty-three were all that stood between him and a gold buckle—first prize at the Louisiana State Fair Rodeo. He could do it and come one step closer to earning a championship title at the National Finals Rodeo in mid-December.

Also at stake today, beating his younger brother Daniel. After three rounds of bull riding over a long, tiring weekend, Daniel currently held the number one spot. Stealing that from him would be icing on a very tasty cake.

"Steady," Daniel said in a low, calming voice that might have been meant for the bull or Jacob. Hard to tell.

His brother straddled the side of the chute, acting as spotter for Jacob, who levered himself above the bull's back, waiting for the exact right moment. When Daniel had taken his run earlier, Jacob spotted him. They might be fierce competitors, but they were also brothers. Close ones. The good and bad circumstances of their lives had created a bond nothing and no one could sever.

Gripping the sides of the chute, Jacob lowered himself one slow inch at a time. The bull, a heavily muscled brute named Gumption, sensed what was coming and kicked the chute wall with a hind leg. The loud bang reverberated in Jacob's ears.

He ignored it. Once in the zone, nothing short of an earthquake would distract him.

Glancing down, he studied the bull and made mental notes. Which way was Gumption looking? Did he paw the ground with his right or left foot? How fast was his breathing?

Jacob had watched the bull perform with

other riders during the first two days of the rodeo. Because of his diligence, he knew Gumption charged straight ahead when released. Jacob would incorporate that important detail into his strategy.

Bull riding, rodeoing in general, was a physical sport. No question of that. But there was also a mental aspect, and it could make the difference between a competitor's leaving with a win or nothing more than a round of sympathetic applause from the audience.

With painstaking care, Jacob settled himself in position on Gumption's back and grabbed the flat braided rope with his right hand. Only a rope. With a cowbell attached for weight. There were no saddles or bridles in bull riding. Letting the rope drop on the off side, he waited for Daniel to reach down and grab it. In addition to spotting, Daniel would "pull the rope" for Jacob, enabling his grip to be as tight as possible. It was a job for only the most trusted.

Gumption's hide twitched as he grew accustomed to this new and unpleasant arrangement. Jacob maneuvered his hand inside the glove until he was satisfied. With his free hand, he pressed his cowboy hat more firmly onto his head.

"Watch him," Daniel warned. "He'll jump once before he starts bucking.

Jacob knew that, too. He didn't answer his brother, however. He rarely spoke while in the zone.

Other faces appeared in his peripheral view. Cowboys hanging on to the railing. They'd pull Jacob off Gumption's back in a heartbeat if the bull suddenly went berserk. It had been known to happen. Bulls were easily riled and unpredictable. That was what made the sport challenging and exciting.

Like the cowboys' faces, the audience in the stands, the bullfighters in the arena, the wranglers manning the gates and the livestock handlers were all a blur. Jacob saw only one thing: the top of Gumption's head.

He waited until the sixth sense that was ingrained in every good bull rider told him the time was right. Then, winging a silent prayer heavenward, he nodded his head, and the chute door flew open.

Gumption charged forward and jumped, as predicted. Because Jacob was ready, he compensated by shifting his weight. The bull came close to unseating him, but Jacob managed to hold on and regain his balance.

Then, the bucking started. The bull's hind

legs reached incredible heights. It was like being trapped inside a cement mixer rotating at top speed. There was a reason Gumption had earned a reputation for being one of the circuit's top bulls. He gave a cowboy the ride of his life, and today was no exception.

Jacob didn't think about the passing seconds. He concentrated on not being thrown and giving the judges a show worth watching. Part of his score depended on how well the bull bucked and how well Jacob rode him.

Gumption abruptly swerved left. Jacob leaned right, his grip on the rope tightening. Every bone in his body felt like it was being ripped loose from its joints. Another change in direction, and Jacob's hat flew off as his head snapped back and forth. He dug his spurs into Gumption's shoulders, urging the bull to buck even higher and earn them the best possible score. Gumption obliged.

Riding bulls never ceased to thrill Jacob. Controlling this kind of power for even a few seconds, facing his fears, was a kick like none other. Hard to believe he'd almost quit rodeoing last year.

Another head-snapping, gut-spinning twist, and the buzzer sounded. Jacob barely heard it. He was more aware of the bullfighters, in their clownlike costumes, diving in, waving their arms and shouting in order to distract the bull. This last part of a cowboy's run could be more dangerous than the ride itself. Bulls sometimes turned on the rider or another bystander without warning.

Drawing a breath, he angled his body sideways and let go of the rope, executing a dismount that more resembled a somersault. By some minor miracle, he landed mostly on his feet and scrambled out from beneath Gumption's thrashing hooves.

The bull gave a few more bucks and twists for good measure before settling down and trotting in circles. He knew his job and that it was over. Soon enough, he was herded to the far end of the arena where the waiting wranglers opened the exit gate for him.

The crowd cheered as one of the bullfighters came over to check on Jacob.

"Good ride, cowboy," he said before performing an antic for the crowd intended to relieve the tension.

Jacob's boots sank into the arena floor as he trudged over to where his hat had fallen. Slapping it against his thigh to dislodge the dirt, he straightened, his gaze automatically going to the scoreboard and the video replay screen. Damn, that was a good ride.

The numbers appeared in big red letters, along with his ranking: 84.5. Not his best score ever, but good enough to land him in first place. As the last rider to compete, the win was officially his.

A wide smile spread across his face. He was going to do it. Earn himself a national title in December. And when he did, Brock would finally give him the promotion at Baron Energies that Jacob deserved.

A hand gripped his shoulder as he exited the arena gate and squeezed.

"Congrats!" Jet Baron greeted him with an enthusiastic grin. "You did it, bro!"

Bro? Try as he might, Jacob couldn't think of himself as Jet's brother. He and Daniel were adopted. Members of the Baron family for nineteen years, yet not members. Their adoptive father, Brock, openly favored his biological children, Jet in particular. As such, Jacob had never really gotten close to Jet and his—*their,* he reminded himself—three sisters.

Rodeoing hadn't helped. Like Daniel, Jacob was in competition with Jet. In fact, as the only licensed pilot in the family, Jet often flew the three of them to events in the family's small Cessna. They'd driven this weekend, however. Shreveport, Louisiana, was only three hours from the family's ranch outside of Dallas—and the ranch wasn't far from Baron Energies headquarters.

"Thanks," Jacob said, accepting a clap on his back from Jet.

By then, he was surrounded. Friends, rivals and Daniel, all eager to congratulate him.

"You didn't do so bad yourself," Jacob told Daniel. "Second place."

"Yeah, but I whipped your ass in saddle bronc riding."

He had. Jacob didn't mind. He'd be taking home first place in two events today, bull riding and, thanks to the loan of a horse from a buddy, steer wrestling. Brock would be pleased.

The brothers hung around for the buckle ceremony at the end of the rodeo and an interview with a local TV station. After that, Jet was raring to head home. Jacob didn't blame him. Jet had a new fiancée waiting for him. Jasmine Carter. An engineer with twin girls.

Another reason to hit the road, their sister Lizzie had recently given birth to the Baron family's first grandchild, a daughter named

Natalie Adele. Jacob felt a bit guilty about leaving town so soon afterward to rodeo. No need, he told himself. He'd made a visit to the hospital to see the baby before they left and brought flowers. In his opinion, the new parents, while elated, seemed frazzled and overwhelmed. They probably didn't need a bunch of relations hanging around and underfoot.

Jacob made a mental note to pick up something from one of the rodeo vendors for his new niece. What size T-shirt did a newborn wear?

"You working tomorrow?" Daniel asked.

"Bright and early."

Jacob's shift at the Eagle started at 6:00 a.m. and ended late, 6:00 p.m. He was the senior safety manager for Baron Energies' largest producing oil well. The extended shifts allowed Jacob to have at least three days off on the weekends to rodeo.

It was a good job, and the flexible schedule a perk, but Jacob wanted more. Specifically, to be head of Baron Energies' yet-to-be-formed alternative energy division.

Brock had flat out refused to consider anything not dealing with oil. Until now. With each gold buckle Jacob brought home, Brock's resistance wavered. He claimed to see potential in Jacob previously hidden. A national title would, Jacob was convinced, break down Brock's resistance entirely.

Thanks to a B-list country singer giving a post-rodeo concert, the arena stands remained packed, and the lines to the food vendors and merchant stalls blocked the midway. Jacob, Daniel and Jet wound their way through the throng of people, saying goodbye to their friends and promising to see their fellow competitors next weekend.

"Excuse me, Jacob Baron?"

At first, Jacob didn't think anything of the unfamiliar voice calling to him. He and his brothers were often approached by female fans.

Then he turned to look at the woman and was immediately taken aback. She looked vaguely familiar, though he couldn't recall where he'd seen her before.

"Jacob Baron?" she repeated.

"Yes." He answered without thinking.

She started toward him, managing to cover the uneven ground gracefully despite her absurdly high heels that had no business being at a rodeo. Neither did the skintight black skirt and jacket she wore. "May I speak to you a moment?" Her glance darted briefly to his brothers before returning to him. "Privately."

This was no fan.

Possibly a reporter, though he didn't think so.

Beside him, Daniel whistled. "Wow."

That was something of an understatement. Out-of-place wardrobe aside, the woman was killer gorgeous. Striking green eyes, long strawberry blonde hair and flawless skin.

The same sixth sense he counted on in bull riding came suddenly alive, and it was warning Jacob to proceed with caution.

"We were just heading home," he said.

"This is important."

After a moment's hesitation he hitched his chin toward the parking area where they'd left their truck. "Go on, I'll catch up with you."

"No rush, bro," Jet said, a glimmer in his eyes. "We'll wait."

Jacob gestured for the woman to lead the way.

She wasted no time locating one of the few empty tables near the row of food vendors. In the arena, the band was setting up on a hastily erected temporary stage.

"It seems you know my name." He gave her a careful smile. "Mind telling me yours?"

"Mariana Snow."

Jacob sat back, feeling as if he'd taken a blow from behind. "I'm sorry about your sister. I heard what happened."

Leah Snow. That explained why he found this woman—Mariana—familiar. Three years ago he'd dated her sister, though describing their one long weekend together as dating was a stretch. He hadn't seen her since. She'd refused his calls and promptly quit barrel racing.

Still, the rodeo world was a small one, and he'd learned of Leah's unexpected passing after a short and intense battle with breast cancer. The news had startled him, and left him empty for weeks. Had that been why she'd refused his phone calls?

"Thank you for your condolences," Mariana said tightly. "It's been a difficult three months."

"I didn't know Leah had a sister. She never mentioned you."

Truthfully, they hadn't talked much during those three days. He'd naturally assumed they'd get to know each other over time, only that hadn't happened. Eventually, he'd written off the weekend as one of those temporary rodeo hookups, the kind he generally avoided.

"I'm not surprised." Mariana reached into the leather purse she'd set on the table. "Leah didn't tell you a lot of things." She extracted a snapshot and handed it across the table to Jacob.

He took the photo, his gaze drawn to the laughing face of a young boy. "I don't understand. Who is this?" He started to return the photo.

Mariana held up her hand. "Keep it."

"Why?"

"That's Cody Snow. Your son."

For a moment, Jacob sat immobile, his mind rebelling. He hadn't been careless. He'd asked and Leah swore she was on birth control pills.

"You're mistaken. I don't have a son."

"Yes, you do. And with my sister gone, you're his one remaining parent."

The photo slipped from Jacob's fingers and landed on the table, the boy's laughing face staring up at him.

Frankly, Mariana was surprised Jacob had agreed to let her drive him home to Dallas. She'd suggested it when the band started playing and conversation became difficult over the noise. She'd give him credit for that. A lot of men might have run the instant she'd pulled out the picture of her nephew.

"I'm parked over here." She pointed to the very last row in the dirt parking lot.

He'd just gotten off the phone with one of his brothers, letting them know he'd be, as he put it, hitching a ride back to Dallas with her. That was all he'd told them, and the message had been delivered through clenched teeth.

She didn't blame him. It was a lot to take in. She hadn't expected him to leap with joy when she sprang the news on him. His willingness to discuss her nephew was actually more than she'd anticipated. Though talk was cheap, as Mariana well knew.

"I apologize for ambushing you at the rodeo and in front of your family," she said. "It was a spur-of-the-moment decision. I was visiting a client here in Shreveport. When I found out you were competing today, I decided to try and find you."

"Did you think I'd refuse to meet you somewhere else?"

"The thought did occur to me," she admitted. "Or that you wouldn't come alone." He was a member of a powerful and influential family, one that employed an army of attorneys and advisers.

"I'm not agreeing to anything without DNA testing."

"Of course."

Mariana had taken her sister's word that Jacob Baron was Cody's father. While unlikely, it was possible Leah had slept with more than one man. As Mariana only recently learned, her sister had been insistent on getting pregnant. Jacob required proof, and she understood that. Were he her client, she'd advise the exact same thing.

Reaching into the side pocket of her purse for her keys, she stumbled when her heel caught in a small hole. These shoes were definitely not made for traipsing across rodeo grounds. Not that she owned a single pair of boots.

Feeling a steadying hand on her elbow, she turned and muttered, "Thank you."

Jacob let his hand linger. "Are you all right?"

"I'm fine. Really." Her ankle did twinge a bit. The sensation was overshadowed by the tingle his touch evoked and the look of appreciation in his eyes. That had startled her more than the stumble.

Withdrawing her arm, she attempted a smile. He was simply being a gentleman, right? Cowboys were like that. Old-fashioned and mannerly. At least, most of the ones who'd traveled in and out of her sister's life were. The same could be said for their father. That was part of his charm and why the ladies loved him.

All the ladies. Even the ones he took up with while he was still married to Mariana's mother.

She depressed the button on her key fob, and her headlights flashed in greeting as the door locks popped open. The Infiniti was a recent purchase. She'd decided if she wanted to make junior partner, she needed to *look* like a junior partner.

Jacob opened the driver's side door for her. It was on the tip of her tongue to object. This wasn't a date. She refrained, however. He was surely just being polite. *Cowboys,* she thought with a sigh.

As they bumped and bounced out of the dirt parking lot, Mariana worried about the paint on her car. What had she been thinking, coming here at the last second? The signs in town advertising the rodeo had been too tempting to resist. More so when a quick phone call confirmed Jacob was competing.

"You mentioned visiting a client. What is it you do?" He didn't appear to mind the rocky ride. Neither did he wince with each scraping sound.

"I'm an attorney with Hasbrough and Colletti."

"Ah." He instantly closed down, as if a steel door slammed shut between them.

"I assure you, I'm not after your money. This is no scam or blackmail scheme. I'm concerned only for my nephew and what's best for him."

"Right."

Mariana took his reaction in stride. She was an attorney, after all, and used to it. Those in her profession were frequently the answer to someone's prayers or their worst nightmare.

They approached the main road, and she released a pent-up breath. Without thinking, she reached out and gave the dash a there-there pat. Jacob raised one eyebrow but said nothing. Once they were on the main road and traffic eased, she was able to concentrate.

"Perhaps I should start at the beginning," she said.

"Please do."

"I didn't know who Cody's father was until right before the doctors put Leah on life support. She never told anyone that I know of. I think she believed she could beat the cancer.

She did once before, four years ago, and our mother's a survivor."

"I didn't realize."

A small, painful lump formed in Mariana's throat. She swallowed before speaking. "Leah gave me your name but begged me not to tell you until Cody was eighteen. She didn't want your money, Mr. Baron. Only to be a mother."

"Call me Jacob. And why are you telling me rather than respecting her wishes?"

"That's a very long story." And Mariana wasn't about to delve into her daddy issues with a complete stranger. "In a nutshell, I believe it's the right thing. Legally and morally. You have a son and should be allowed a role in his life. He deserves all the benefits a father can provide."

"A role?"

"However great or small a role you choose."

With his schedule, she doubted he'd want more than every other weekend, if that. Didn't rodeo cowboys like him want their freedom? That was what her father told her mother right before he walked out on them.

"Noble of you." Jacob's voice rang with suspicion.

"We've just met. You have no reason to trust

me. Especially with the bombshell I've just dropped."

"Bombshell, yeah," he said drily.

"But you will see soon enough that my intentions are indeed noble."

"I'm guessing Leah named you as his guardian or something."

"She did. She also put your name as father on Cody's birth certificate. You're his legal father. DNA testing will reveal if you're his biological father, as well."

"You say she told you right before she was put on life support?"

"Yes. The circumstances were grave. I don't think she was lying."

Jacob leaned his head back and rubbed a spot on his forehead as if it throbbed.

Mariana was momentarily struck by his ruggedly handsome profile, which was not at all like her. Broad shoulders didn't sway her. Neither did dark, penetrating eyes and a mouth that could only be described as sexy.

Had she really just thought that? Yes, she had, and she needed to stop right this second. It wasn't easy. Jacob drew her glance like a magnet.

He'd been smiling when she first spotted him at the rodeo, and to her chagrin, her heart had given a small leap. He was staring out the windshield now, and his intense expression was nearly as captivating as his smile. No wonder Leah had chosen Jacob to father her child.

Probably best not to bring up that little tidbit. Hard enough learning he was a father. Finding out Leah had used him merely as a sperm donor…well, it wasn't necessary and was too risky. She didn't want to give him a reason to abandon Cody entirely. Her conscience wouldn't let her.

Running a background check on Jacob wasn't something Mariana had immediately done once Leah revealed his name. Rather, she and her mother had stayed by Leah's side as the machines kept her alive. They'd said their goodbyes, made their peace and let her hold Cody in the crook of her frail arm. Her eventual passing was poignant and gutwrenching.

With it also came a certain amount of relief. Leah was no longer in pain. After a small but moving memorial service, Mariana became the mother figure in Cody's life. It was a role she'd gladly fulfill indefinitely.

Depending on what Jacob wanted to do, it was also a role she might be forced to give up. Mariana had wrestled over telling him for weeks.

She and her sister had never agreed on a father's responsibility toward his children. Leah believed as their mother did: a man was unnecessary and would ultimately break your heart. Mariana felt the complete opposite. Fathers had a moral responsibility to their children as well as a fiscal one. Her profession only reinforced that in her mind.

Shortly after the memorial service, she began accumulating information on Jacob. No way would she allow him visitation, much less share custody of her nephew, should he be unfit.

Jacob certainly had the means to support a son. He was from a wealthy family, was college educated, held a good position as senior safety manager at Baron Energies' largest drill site—though she was surprised he wasn't further up the food chain—owned his own home and was, by all accounts, an upstanding citizen.

He had only one fault in her opinion, and it was a doozy. Rodeoing. Besides the frequent nomadic lifestyle, there were also buckle bunnies. A man with Jacob's good looks was bound to have a vast following, though from Mariana's research, he didn't avail himself.

Except, apparently, for her sister. Though by her own admission, Leah had misled him.

Mariana's sense of right and wrong had eventually prevailed, and she decided to approach Jacob. She just hadn't planned on it being today. Maybe she should have curbed her impulses when those signs for the rodeo appeared.

"Please don't feel that I'm pressuring you into anything," she said to him. "We'll take this one step at a time at whatever speed you're comfortable."

"If he is my son, I'll do the right thing."

"Good. We're in agreement on that."

Mariana didn't jump for joy. She'd heard fathers make similar statements before, then go back on their word. If that happened, she was prepared to raise Cody herself. More than prepared, she was happy to. She loved her nephew.

She turned from the road onto the freeway. It had grown dark since they left the rodeo grounds. Jacob's face was cast in shadows. Mariana allowed herself to relax. She wouldn't be distracted by him for the remainder of the trip home.

"What's the first step?" he asked, the edge in his voice unmistakable. "Meeting him?"

"We start with the DNA testing. I can give you the name of a facility my firm uses. It's downtown, not far from Baron Energies' offices. Or we can use one of your own choosing."

"Is there one in southwest Dallas? The farther south and west the better. I can drive over at lunch tomorrow."

He wanted a facility near the drill site where he worked. That made sense.

"If you give me your phone number when I drop you off, I'll research a location and text you the info tomorrow morning after I arrange for the testing. You can go in at your convenience. But if you'd be kind enough to let me know when you do, I'd appreciate it."

"Okay."

"It's a very simple and quick procedure."

"How long? For the results," he clarified.

"Five to seven business days. You'll be notified by email when the results are available and—"

"Okay," he said again in a tone that clearly implied he was through discussing the testing.

Again, she cut him some slack. This was an enormous amount to process. She must be patient.

Several minutes of silence followed, after which he asked, "Then what?"

"If the results are positive, we can set up a meeting for you and Cody."

"Who's taking care of him now? Seeing as you're here."

That wasn't a question she'd expected from him. "He's in day care during the week when I'm at work. Today, my mother's watching him. She lives in Austin and drives up every other weekend."

"How does she feel about this? You telling me."

Another unexpected question. Mariana relied on the skills she acquired as an attorney to maintain her composure and smiled. "She doesn't know."

"She doesn't approve."

Jacob was obviously more astute than she'd first thought.

"She loves Cody very much, and he's all she has left of Leah." The painful lump returned, forcing Mariana to wait before speaking. "I decided not to tell her until you and I had talked and the DNA results are in. Why upset the apple cart for no reason?"

Several more minutes of silence passed. Mariana was ready to spend the remainder of the ride with only her own thoughts for company when Jacob spoke softly from the darkness.

"Tell me about him. Cody. What's he's like?"

For the first time since she'd approached him on the rodeo midway, she began to think Jacob might have an interest in Cody.

She described her charming yet headstrong nephew until the next exit on the freeway, when Jacob's lack of response caused her earlier doubts to return. If he turned out to be like Mariana's father, then poor little Cody would be the one to pay the price.

Chapter 2

The noise was constant and nearly deafening, even with earplugs. Jacob didn't remove the small foam devices until he was far from the drill site, stuffing them into the front pocket of his work shirt. He could still hear the rig and the generators grinding in the distance. Sometimes, he thought he could hear them in his sleep.

His hard hat came off next, and he ran fingers through his perpetually damp hair. The drill site was in a constant state of sweltering, summer, winter, spring and fall. In addition to noise, the massive drill gave off enormous amounts of heat. Today, Mother Nature added to their discomfort by providing unseasonably warm weather for early November.

Jacob opened the door to his truck, tossing his hard hat and fluorescent-green vest onto the passenger seat. His aim was good—or bad, depending on one's perspective. The hat hit a stack of papers and hand tools, knocking them onto the floorboard. He didn't bother straightening the mess.

I'm a father. Could be a father, he amended. He'd find out for sure when the test results came back in roughly a week. As Mariana mentioned, he'd receive an email with a link to the lab's secure website where he could log in and view the results.

One email, and his life could be forever changed in ways he had only begun to imagine.

Jacob lived twenty minutes from the drill site and twenty-five minutes from Baron Energies' headquarters in Dallas. Convenient. He'd bought the house last year, planning on being promoted from the field to an executive position. That had yet to happen.

Brock refused to consider transferring Jacob. Not until he'd "gained more experience." In truth, Brock had been waiting and hoping for Jet, his biological son, to take an interest in the company. Jet had finally started coming around, leaving Jacob even further out in the cold.

Every proposal he presented, and he did it often, was immediately shot down with Brock proclaiming in a loud voice, "There will be no alternate energy division. Not as long as I'm in charge. We Barons are oil people."

How anyone could look at the world today and not recognize the value of alternate energy baffled Jacob. Oil was a limited resource. Wind and sun weren't. For at least the next billion years.

Out of frustration and anger, Jacob had returned to rodeoing this past spring, seeking an outlet for his pent-up energy. No pun intended. It had been a great stress reliever and, at first, fun. Then he'd started winning, and— this was a surprise—Brock had taken notice.

The higher Jacob's ranking climbed, the more frequent talks he and his adoptive father engaged in about Jacob's future with the company. Brock was still determined that Jet take over one day—now it was alongside his sister Lizzie. But he was listening to, if not entirely agreeing with, Jacob's ideas for expansion.

To that end, Jacob spent every weekend on the road or in the air. It had paid off. He was a hairbreadth away from qualifying for the

National Finals Rodeo in December. Brock was thrilled. He himself had won a few titles back in the day. Carly, too. Jacob would be the first of his sons to follow in his footsteps.

Maybe follow. How would a son affect Jacob's career? Both of his careers?

Visitation or custody? Mariana Snow hadn't been specific as to which. He still thought it a little strange that she didn't want full custody herself. If she hadn't told Jacob, he might never have known he had a son. She could have easily complied with her sister's wishes, and Jacob would have been none the wiser. It was enough to give him pause.

Rather than head directly home, he drove to the family ranch. The Roughneck was a little out of the way but worth it. Days like this one, he needed to climb on the back of a horse. In his opinion, there was no better way to work off stress or unload a heavy mind.

It was well past dark when he arrived. That wouldn't be a problem. Floodlights were scattered throughout the barn and arena. He could ride for an hour and still be home by eight.

He maneuvered his truck into the long driveway, noting the darkened farm store as he passed it. His adoptive sisters Savannah and Carly ran the store, which offered fresh produce and homemade pies. The two had recently embarked on a search for their biological mother, Delia Baron, with only dead ends and cold trails to show for their efforts.

Jacob didn't need to search for his biological father. He knew right where Oscar Burke resided: the Federal Correctional Institute in Beaumont. Minimum security, as if that counted for anything. This February, he'd be up for parole. The third time. Had he not been involved in an attack against a guard—an innocent bystander, he claimed; the perpetrator, witnesses had testified—he'd be out by now.

Jacob pulled in next to the barn and parked. The main lights were on. Since he was the only one who ever rode at night, that meant Luke Nobel, the Roughneck's ranch manager and Carly's fiancé, was dealing with a problem.

Jacob found Luke in the barn, his forearms propped on a stall door and staring worriedly at the horse inside.

"What's wrong?"

"Colic."

The smile Jacob would normally expect to see on Luke's face was absent.

"Not good."

For a few minutes they discussed the mare's symptoms and what steps Luke had taken.

"If she isn't better in an hour, I'm calling the vet."

The large chestnut stood with her head hanging low between her front legs and her eyes filled with misery.

"You sure you want to wait that long? This horse is one of Brock's favorites."

Luke shrugged. "I'll keep a close watch on her." If necessary, he'd climb into the stall with the mare. "You going for a ride?" He glanced pointedly at the change of clothes and pair of boots in Jacob's hands.

"Thinking of taking Zeus out for a spin."

The gelding was the horse Jacob had used for calf roping and steer wrestling, two rodeo events he enjoyed but had mostly stopped competing in. His four twelve-hour shifts at the drill site left him with just enough time on the weekends to get to whatever rodeo he was competing in. Trailering a horse would be too time-consuming. As a result, Jacob focused solely on bucking events, with the occasional steer wrestling thrown in.

"I'd join you if I could," Luke said.

"You have your priorities."

The two were good friends and had been for years. They'd competed against each other on the circuit until Luke retired from rodeoing to care for his daughter who, Jacob just that moment realized, was about the same age as Cody. Now, Luke was marrying Jacob's sister Carly.

Fatherhood and family life suited his friend. Would it suit Jacob? What kind of father would he be? Lord knows, Oscar Burke was a poor excuse and no role model. And Brock, while better, treated Jacob and Daniel differently from his own children.

Not once had he ever told Jacob that he loved him. Might be because he didn't.

For a lot of years, that hurt. No more. Not that he'd admit.

"What's on your mind?" Luke asked, giving Jacob the once-over.

Was he that transparent? "Just because I'm going for a ride doesn't mean I'm wrestling with a problem."

Luke shrugged. "Except you are."

Okay, he *was* that transparent. "Do you miss rodeoing?"

"Sure I do. Once in a while."

"Would you go back if you could?"

"Probably getting a little too long in the tooth."

Jacob understood. At twenty-eight, the majority of men he competed against were younger than him.

"You're not thinking of quitting?" Luke asked.

Jacob shook his head. "Not this year. Now, if I win a title or two…"

"You'll be too busy pushing papers at Baron Energies to ride bulls."

"I hope to do a lot more than push papers." Like take the company into the next decade.

"Brock softening any?"

"He's hinted that he might be willing to look at a new proposal after the first of the year." Which translated into after the National Finals Rodeo. "I've been keeping my ear to the ground. Rumors are circulating that Starr Solar Systems is coming up for sale."

Luke chuckled. "The accident must have had more of an effect on the old man than we thought."

Brock had suffered a terrible fall earlier in the year while competing in a senior pro rodeo. The injury to his leg had confined him to a wheelchair for months, and he'd been forced to relinquish the day-to-day running of Baron Energies to Lizzie, his oldest daughter.

Savannah and Carly supervised his care at home, an arrangement that had driven everyone crazy. Brock had always possessed a bigger-than-life personality and the physical stamina to match. Luckily, he was well on the path to recovery and had very recently returned to Baron's boardroom on a part-time basis.

"That," Jacob mused aloud, "and his kids are all getting married."

What were the odds the Baron siblings had each recently found their match?

"Don't forget Lizzie," Luke said. "Grandchildren can change a person. It did my parents."

Grandchildren! Lizzie had just delivered Brock's first, and he crowed his delight to anyone who'd listen.

Except if Jacob was Cody's father, then, technically, the boy would be Brock's first and oldest.

Adoptive grandchild. Not the same. Jacob had no reason to believe Brock would treat Cody any differently than he'd treated Jacob and Daniel their whole lives. The thought left a bitter taste in his mouth.

"I wouldn't trade my life for anything." Luke flashed his previously missing smile. "Nothing is more satisfying than coming home to Rosie and Carly. Not work, not rodeoing, not anything."

"I've never given much thought to getting

married and having kids." Tired of holding his boots, Jacob set them on the ground and laid his clothes on top.

"You need to make your mark in the world first."

Less making his mark and more proving he was as good as any Baron, regardless of his start in life and his father's criminal history, though Jacob didn't say it out loud.

"You must still miss your mom." Compassion filled Luke's voice.

"Every day."

Seven years ago. Peggy Burke Baron had gone into the hospital for a routine appendectomy and come through the surgery with flying colors. She'd died a week later from a staph infection, leaving her two sons without a mother and her second husband a widower.

Jacob still felt the loss keenly. Brock not so much. Less than two years later, he remarried. Julieta was thirty years his junior and the mother of a little boy. Jacob's adoptive siblings all adored Julieta and her son. She was nice enough, and the kid was okay, Jacob supposed. But that was the extent of his feelings.

He wasn't jealous exactly. He might have been only nine when Brock and his mother wed, but he'd figured out soon after that their marriage was based on convenience and affection. Not love. But marrying so quickly after his mother's death and to a significantly younger and beautiful woman felt like an insult.

Luke squeezed Jacob's shoulder. "She was a fine lady with a heart of gold. She'd be proud of you."

Jacob had a sobering thought. If Leah's son was his, the boy would never meet either of Jacob's parents. Only Brock.

"Do you remember Leah Snow?" he asked.

Luke scratched behind an ear. "Vaguely. A barrel racer, right?"

"She died a few months ago. From breast cancer."

"Oh, man. That's a shame."

"She and I dated a few years ago."

"You never said anything."

"It was brief. A weekend." Jacob gathered his courage. He'd decided not to tell anyone about Cody until the DNA test results were in and only if they were positive. Suddenly, he wanted someone to know. "Her sister, Mariana Snow, approached me at the Louisiana State Fair Rodeo. It seems Leah has a son."

"Really."

"She told Mariana before she died that I was the father."

"Wow." Luke looked as stunned as Jacob had felt upon hearing the news.

"Yeah."

"Are you?"

"I'll know for sure soon." Jacob exhaled a long breath. There was both relief in the telling and increased anxiety. "But it's pretty likely."

"What are you going to do?" Luke asked.

"Mariana wants me to be a part of the boy's life."

"What does that mean?"

"Not sure, she didn't say. Visitation. Custody maybe."

"And you're not sure how you feel about that," Luke stated.

"I can barely handle work and rodeoing. How am I supposed to take care of a two-year-old? Even part-time. I don't know the first thing."

"No parent does in the beginning. But we learn."

"You're a natural father."

"And you're worried about the sacrifices you'll have to make."

Jacob squeezed his eyes shut, feeling completely out of control and at the mercy of the fates.

"I've worked so hard for years to get ahead. Finally, I have a chance at a championship title and a promotion. Now this." He stopped abruptly. "I sound like a selfish bastard."

"There isn't a parent alive who doesn't wonder about the impact children will have on their future."

"What if I'm not cut out to be a dad? It's not like I've had the best examples."

"The better question might be what if you are?"

Though Jacob admired his friend greatly, he couldn't conceive of sacrificing everything he'd worked so hard for.

"What if I just offered financial support? At least until after Finals? That's only six weeks away."

Luke didn't hide his disappointment. "Now you sound just like Brock."

Nothing his friend said or did could have made a bigger impact on Jacob. He did sound like Brock *and* his biological father.

Disgust filled him. "I guess the apple doesn't fall far from the tree."

"It does." Luke leaned an elbow on the stall door, his gaze direct. "You aren't like either Brock or your father. At least, you don't have to be."

Cody's photo, tucked in his wallet, burned a hole in Jacob's back pocket. The boy deserved a better father than he'd had. The best Jacob could be.

"I always swore if I ever had children, I'd do right by them."

Luke grinned. "Here's your chance."

"I'm still waiting for the DNA results."

"That's wise."

The hour ride on Zeus helped to further clear Jacob's head and give him purpose. After returning the gelding to its stall, he started for his truck. At the door, he paused and took out his cell phone. Mariana had given him her number yesterday. He dialed it now.

"This is Jacob," he said when she answered. "I want to meet Cody. Tomorrow."

"We're here," Mariana announced in a singsong voice as they neared Jacob's house.

She'd been driving down the street at ten miles an hour, peering at address numbers posted above garage doors or on wrought iron gates. It was a nice, middle-class neighborhood. Most of the attractive homes were on large lots with drought-resistant natural landscaping.

"Daddy, Daddy!" Cody expressed his delight by tossing his stuffed pony in the air. It hit the back of Mariana's seat and bounced off. "Wanna see Daddy."

"We will." She maneuvered the SUV into the driveway and parked. The vehicle belonged to her mother. Much more appropriate for transporting a toddler than her Infiniti. "Cool your jets."

"Jets!" Cody kicked his sneakered feet wildly, and they banged into the console dividing the front seats.

"Okay, Cody. That's enough." She kept her voice level but firm.

Her nephew stopped. For an entire three seconds. "Wanna see Daddy," he repeated and resumed kicking.

She'd thought it best to wait for the test results to come in before telling Cody he had a father. Somehow, he'd gleaned enough while listening to Mariana and her mother talking about Jacob to realize he had one of those magical, mystical beings: a father.

Served her right for having a supersmart nephew. Or, possibly, daddies were spoken of frequently at day care. He'd surely seen them picking up his playmates. That would explain his fascination. Wanting his and Jacob's initial meeting to go well, Mariana had infused brightness into her voice when she talked about Jacob. As a result, Cody's excitement soared.

Jacob had phoned her yesterday and insisted on meeting Cody, to Mariana's surprise. She'd tried to convince him to wait, without success. He'd been adamant, and she didn't want to give him a reason to bring in his attorneys or, worse, flee.

Errant fathers weren't her specialty at the law firm where she worked. She did, however, have some experience with them. Her mother had spent years chasing down Mariana and Leah's father, who never stayed in one place longer than a few months. When her mother did find him, there was a guaranteed battle over past due child support.

Mariana was twenty-nine years old, and her mother had yet to receive all the money owed her. The SOB didn't even have the decency to show up at Leah's memorial service.

She could understand her sister's not wanting a man like that to be a part of her son's life. But Jacob Baron wasn't cut from the same cloth. Mariana knew; she'd done her homework on him *and* his family. He could, and hopefully would, do right by Cody.

Leah had also done her homework before

selecting Jacob. Still, despite his many worthy attributes, she'd insisted on raising her son alone, even after the cancer returned and progressed at a terrifying rate.

Mariana stared at the pickup truck in the driveway, uncertainty gnawing away at her. If only he wasn't a rodeo man like her father, she'd feel a whole lot better. At least he had a good, *steady* job and belonged to a family with deep roots in the Dallas area. That compensated for some of his less desirable cowboy traits.

Her cell phone rang just as she turned off the ignition.

"Yes, Helena," she said after her secretary identified herself.

"Sorry to bother you this late, but I thought you'd want to know now rather than in the morning."

Mariana braced herself. "What is it?"

"Paulo Molinas's attorney has filed a motion to suppress Medallion Investments' phone records."

"Dammit," she muttered, then glanced over her shoulder. Had Cody heard her curse? She didn't think so. "All right. Pull the former case files we talked about and leave them on my desk for the morning."

"Will do."

They discussed a few more details before ending the call. Mariana tried to focus on Cody and his introduction to Jacob. It took all her effort. Her firm's joint lawsuits had gained momentum in recent weeks. Ten-hour days made caring for Cody challenging. She was lucky to have gotten off early.

That *wasn't* the reason she wanted Jacob to have shared custody of Cody, she told herself for the hundredth time. Her workload and demanding schedule had *nothing* to do with it.

Opening the rear passenger side door, she bent over Cody and unbuckled him from the car seat.

"Daddy, Daddy! Where Daddy?"

She winced at the loud voice inches from her ear. "Shhh. We'll see him in a minute."

"I firsty."

"We'll get you a drink inside."

This constant speaking in the plural amazed her. She couldn't recall thinking about it, only doing it. Was that normal? Did every mother, or aunt or guardian, naturally fall into the habit?

Lifting Cody from the car, she set him on his feet and grabbed the overstuffed diaper bag.

"Wait a minute," she said when he started

squirming. Setting the diaper bag down, she adjusted his little denim jacket, re-fastening the buttons that had mysteriously come loose during the ride.

She'd have preferred Cody wear something newer and without a hole in the left sleeve. But this particular jacket was his favorite, and he'd pitched a fit when she tried to put him in a hooded sweatshirt. Even his favorite cartoon character on the front hadn't swayed him.

He would have run ahead if not for her firm grip on his hand. As it was, he pulled her and the diaper bag along like a heavy anchor through water.

"Slow down, honey," Mariana admonished.

The house, a newer one-story with tan stucco exterior and—this was good—a block fence enclosing the rear yard, sat on a corner lot. Hopefully, Jacob didn't own a pool. Toddlers and water were a dangerous combination.

Mariana thought it interesting that he didn't live at the Roughneck, his family's ranch. The place was certainly big enough. Then again, this house was closer to the drill site where he worked. Or maybe he simply liked his privacy.

If he assumed any level of custody, he'd

soon lose that luxury. There was no such thing as privacy with a two-year-old in the house. If presented with a closed door or locked cabinet, Cody felt compelled to holler until it opened or his lungs gave out.

Her high heels wobbled as they walked along the slate rock path leading to the front door. Changing clothes beforehand would have been nice. There'd been no time, however. Mariana was barely able to rush from the office to day care, navigate traffic and still make it here—she glanced at her watch—twelve minutes late.

Jacob opened the door seconds after she rang the bell. Had he been watching from the window?

"Hello," he said in a neutral voice, his gaze meeting hers briefly before traveling to Cody where it remained. "Come in."

"Thank you." She required a moment to collect her wits.

He looked good. His short dark hair appeared freshly combed, and the scent of soap clung to him as if he'd recently washed up. Like her, he hadn't changed from work. His pale blue chambray shirt had a Baron Energies logo embroidered on the front pocket and the sleeves were rolled up to reveal strong, muscled forearms.

Mariana was beginning to think he could dress in a ratty T-shirt and gym shorts and she'd still be affected. How might he look in, say, a suit? Or, better yet, a tuxedo?

She wagged a mental finger at herself, warning her mind not to go there. Theirs was a business meeting. Of sorts, anyway. There were certainly business matters to discuss.

"This is Cody." She propelled the boy ahead of her, realizing only then that he'd stopped jabbering.

In fact, his small mouth literally hung open, and he stared up at Jacob with enormous eyes.

"How do you do, pal?" Jacob smiled. If one could call the thin slash splitting the lower half of his face a smile.

Was he nervous? Angry? Shy? Distrustful? All of the above?

Cody suddenly flung himself at Mariana, hugging her legs with all his strength, and whimpered.

"It's all right, honey."

She stroked his downy soft hair, not noticing until right that moment how much it resembled Jacob's. Only a shade lighter. The shape of his face was similar, too. As was the color of his eyes.

"I didn't know if you might be hungry." Jacob started through the living room.

Mariana and a reluctant Cody followed. "Cody can always eat. He's not fussy like some kids." Actually, Mariana didn't know anything about other kids. She was repeating her mother's frequent declarations. "I'm not really hungry."

She spoke too soon. The moment they entered the kitchen, a delicious aroma had her practically drooling. When was the last time she'd eaten a meal that wasn't takeout or purchased in the frozen food aisle of the grocery store?

"You cook?" she blurted without thinking, then could have kicked herself for being rude.

"I got home a little early. Figured if I was hungry, you and Cody might be, too."

"One of us had animal crackers on the drive over."

"Can I take that for you?" He reached for the diaper bag, and their fingers brushed.

He didn't pull immediately away. Mariana glanced up to find him staring at her. Instantly, her mouth went dry. Oh, boy.

"Mariana."

"Yes?"

The corners of his mouth tipped up. "Let go of the handle."

"Oops. Sorry." She watched him stow the diaper bag on the floor just around the corner, her cheeks hot with embarrassment. Men didn't do this to her. She didn't let them.

Pretending nothing was amiss, she said, "You have a nice place."

"Thanks."

The house wasn't huge, but comfortable and tastefully decorated. Also tidy. Tidier even than her house. Seems Jacob was Mr. Homemaker.

Yeah, well, wait till Cody worked his toddler magic. She considered warning Jacob to enjoy the clean while it lasted.

All at once, Cody squealed with delight. Pulling his hand free of Mariana's, he scrambled toward the table and what lay beneath it. "Puppy, puppy."

It was then Mariana spotted the dog. "Cody, come back." She flung herself forward, arms outstretched. For all she knew, the dog was a vicious brute.

"It's okay," Jacob said. "Buster's used to kids."

The dog raised his head to stare at Cody, who dropped to his hands and knees in order to crawl between the chairs.

"Are you sure?" Mariana fretted, ready to put herself between her nephew and any danger.

"He's a retired show dog. Buster's given more than two thousand performances all over the country. Mostly at rodeos and fund-raisers. But also schools and children's wards at hospitals."

As Mariana watched, Buster gave Cody's face a thorough licking. The boy went insane with happiness and launched into a rapid-fire, one-sided conversation only he could understand.

"What exactly does a show dog do?" she asked, her eyes still glued on Cody.

"Tricks. I'll show you after dinner." Jacob reached into the cupboard for plates. "Though his repertoire isn't what it used to be. Buster's lost almost all his hearing."

"He doesn't look old."

"He's not really. Only eight. Just one of those things." Flatware and salad bowls accompanied the plates. "I'm friends with his former owner and handler. Met the guy years ago on the circuit. He has a new dog now and travels a lot. Buster was left home alone."

"You travel a lot," Mariana commented.

"This year, I have. The girl next door watches Buster. Sometimes I think he loves her more than me."

A two-year-old boy wasn't like a dog. He

couldn't leave Cody in the neighbor girl's care when he went on the road.

Mariana concentrated on slowing her thoughts. Just because she and Cody were there was no reason to jump to conclusions. Jacob hadn't mentioned anything about custody.

He opened the oven door and removed a steaming casserole pan. "I fixed chicken. Figured everyone likes that. Am I wrong?"

"Cody loves chicken, though he needs his portion cut into bite-size pieces."

He set the platter in the center of the table. There were also chunks of roasted potatoes and carrots in with the chicken. "Come and get it."

"Afraid I'm not much of a cook."

"Maybe over dinner you can tell me what you are good at." He flashed her a smile, this time a genuine one. Mariana's heart went pitter-patter.

To hide her disconcertment, she stooped down and retrieved Cody from beneath the table. He refused at first and started screaming, "Puppy, puppy."

Before she could have a little talk with him, Jacob said, "Come here, Buster," and slapped his thigh.

Instantly, the dog sprang to his feet and ambled over to Jacob. Cody chased after him and was caught by Mariana.

Show-off, she thought. Aloud, she said, "I didn't bring his high chair."

"What about a stack of phone books?"

"I don't know. Cody can be squiggly and wiggly."

He made a liar of her. Next to the dog, sitting at the table with the adults was the obvious highlight of his day. He also ate all his food and drank all his milk, copying Jacob.

Mariana didn't know whether to be glad or annoyed. She'd been outdone by a complete novice.

What other surprises did he have in store for her? Something told her Jacob was full of them.

Chapter 3

"Would you like to see the outside?" Jacob gestured toward the French doors leading to the back patio.

"Sure." Mariana smiled politely.

He hadn't yet broached the subject of visitation, wanting to ease into it. A tour of the house seemed like a good starting point. As they'd gone from room to room he felt like a private standing nervously by while the general conducted his inspection. She seemed satisfied, other than the fact that he was lacking child protection devices. A *lot* of them, apparently. Outlet covers. Cabinet locks. Baby gates. The list went on and on.

She'd assured him all the items needed could be easily purchased and installed. If he didn't have the time, a service could be hired to handle it.

A service? Jacob was impressed. *What will they think of next?*

He flipped on the patio light, and Mariana stepped outside. Her gaze traveled the yard.

"No pool," she said with obvious relief.

"I've been considering putting one in." At her horrified gasp, he asked, "Don't kids like pools?"

"Toddlers should never be around water."

"I guess I can wait a few years."

"That's a good idea."

Man, she was obsessive-compulsive where Cody was concerned. Or he was completely ignorant when it came to young children.

Okay, guilty as charged. And given that Leah had recently passed, Mariana's overreacting really wasn't unreasonable.

The subject of their discussion was still enamored with Buster and paying no attention to the adults. He walked alongside the Queensland heeler, his small hand resting on Buster's neck. Periodically, he bent and whispered into the dog's ear or kissed the top of his head. Jacob admitted it was kind of cute.

"Is that a corral?" Mariana peered at the back of the property.

Uh-oh. She had that look on her face again. What had Jacob done wrong now? "I have a full acre, so I built a paddock and a couple covered stalls."

"You have horses?"

"One horse. Amigo. I keep my working horses at the Roughneck and ride there. Amigo is retired. He was my first horse when my mom married Brock. I take him out about once a week for old time's sake."

She tilted her head. "A retired show dog *and* a retired horse?"

"What can I say? I have soft spot."

"That's nice." The warmth in her voice was a pleasant change.

"Cody can ride Amigo if he'd like."

"No riding."

"Not tonight," he agreed. "Another day."

"He's too little. And horses run off."

Well, that didn't last long. Mariana was back to bearing her mother-grizzly-bear teeth.

"Amigo's crippled in his back legs and couldn't run off if he tried. A slow walk is the most I can get out of him."

"Absolutely not," she stated firmly.

For some reason, her bossy attitude rankled

Jacob. Cody was his son. Didn't that give him say in what the kid could and couldn't do?

Jacob opened his mouth to speak, then promptly shut it. The feelings to nurture and protect that had started yesterday while at the Roughneck were growing stronger and stronger. He had a responsibility, and he'd assume it gladly and without reservation. But shouldn't he also feel love? An automatic and unbreakable bond between the two of them like the one Luke shared with Rosie?

Jacob studied Cody, who was still lavishing affection on Buster, and guilt pricked at him. This was the child he'd fathered. What was wrong with him?

Maybe they just needed more time together. The idea made sense. A lot of sense.

The three of them returned inside after a short walk around the yard. Jacob won back some lost points by having a large grassy lawn that Mariana proclaimed was perfect for playing.

"I could install a swing set," he suggested.

"When he's older."

Of course. Why had he even asked?

She was a puzzle, and he found his attention drifting away from Cody and toward her. She wore another suit, except this one had pants rather than a skirt. Too bad. Jacob was a confirmed leg man, and despite the stress that marked their initial meeting, he'd noticed her legs, which were long and shapely enough to appear in a bathing suit ad.

He'd like to see her in a bathing suit. A bikini. Maybe one day soon he could suggest they all three go swimming at the Roughneck. The pool was heated year-round.

On second thought, she probably wouldn't allow Cody within a mile of the pool. Not unless it was drained of water.

Inside, Mariana offered to wash the dishes. "It's only fair since you cooked."

Jacob saw an opportunity and took it. "Great. Cody and I will get acquainted."

"O…kay."

Before she could protest, Jacob took Cody into the family room. Buster and Cody both, that was. The kid wouldn't go two feet without the dog.

There, Jacob sat on the couch and called Buster over. His ploy worked. Cody came, too.

"Watch this," he said and waved his hand in front of Buster's face. It was a technique he used to get the deaf dog's attention. "Green ball."

Instantly, Buster dashed over to a wicker basket in the corner of the room filled with dog toys. He stuck his nose in the basket and came up with a bright green tennis ball, which he brought back to Jacob.

Cody stared in amazement.

"That's nothing," Jacob said and told Buster, "monkey."

The dog dashed off again to the toy basket and brought back a stuffed monkey with one arm and one eye missing. Buster was a little hard on his toys.

"Okay, here we go." As Cody watched, Jacob set both the ball and the monkey on the floor in front of Buster. The dog sat and stared intently but didn't move. "Buster, if I say three, you pick up the ball. If I say four, you pick up the monkey. Ready?"

Thump, thump, thump. The dog's wagging tail hit the floor.

"Seven, nine, one, sixteen, twelve." Jacob looked at Cody and winked. The boy couldn't count, but he seemed entertained. "Ten, four."

Buster snatched up the monkey in the blink of an eye.

Cody burst into laughter.

"Good dog." Jacob patted Buster's head. "Tell him he's a good dog."

Cody patted Buster as Jacob had done and said, "Good dog," over and over.

A tug pulled at Jacob's heart. It was admittedly tiny, but definitely there and something to build on.

He showed the boy a few more of Buster's tricks, finishing with a display of Buster's vocalizing abilities.

"Say hello," Jacob commanded, and the dog yowled comically.

"That's amazing," Mariana said.

Hearing the warmth in her voice, Jacob glanced up. The matching warmth in her expression had him unable to stop staring. She was more than pretty, she was compelling, and the effect she had on him was potent.

"I can't take any of the credit," he said. "My friend trained him."

She came over and petted Buster. "I bet he was something to see."

"If you go onto YouTube and search his name, you'll find a few videos from his heyday. They're fun to watch."

"I just might do that." She moved to the couch and sat next to Jacob. "We can't stay much longer. Cody's bedtime is eight."

"Thanks for bringing him by."

"I think it went well."

"Before you go, can we spend a few minutes discussing visitation?"

"Oh." She abruptly tensed. "Don't you want to wait for the DNA test results?"

"That's a week away, at most."

Sensing his performance was over, Buster stretched out at Jacob's feet. Cody tumbled on top of the dog, whose only reaction was a soft grunt.

"Have you told your family yet about Cody?" she asked.

"Like you, I was waiting. I mentioned him to a friend the other day." Jacob turned the tables on her. "Have you told your mother?"

There was a slight flicker in her expression and then she finally said, "Yes."

"How did she take it?"

"She's concerned for Cody's welfare. Please don't take that wrong. It's nothing against you personally."

"I don't. I'm a complete stranger. Perhaps she and I can also meet. In fact, I'd like that."

"Eventually."

Again, her tone rubbed him the wrong way. "Wow, she must be really upset. Is she going to fight me?"

"There's nothing to fight. You haven't been proven to be an unfit father."

"I'm not any kind of a father."

"Which is one of the reasons I'd prefer to start with weekly supervised visits. Like tonight. Then, we could progress to unsupervised visits. After a few months, you could take Cody for a whole day."

If her expression weren't so serious, he'd think she was joking. "Am I a criminal?"

"What?"

"You're treating me like one. Supervised visits?"

"This is going to a big adjustment for Cody. Moving too fast will only confuse him, and he's already suffered so much."

"I get big adjustments, Mariana. My mother married Brock Baron when I was nine, and my life changed completely. I promise you I'll be sensitive to Cody's needs."

"I'm sure you will. But he's only two."

"And he'll probably adjust a lot faster than a nine-year-old. Look at him." Both their glances traveled to Cody, who lay snuggled beside Buster, the thumb of one hand shoved in his mouth and the fingers of his other hand entwined in the dog's thick fur. "Does he look like he's struggling?"

"It might be a different story if I weren't here."

"Why are you backpedaling all of a sudden?"

Her lips thinned. "I'm not."

"You came to me. You suggested I have a role in Cody's life, to whatever extent I choose."

"After an adjustment period."

"According to you, a very long adjustment period. Did your mother change your mind?"

"My mother does have reservations and raised some valid points. After considering them, I reviewed my original position."

Always the carefully worded answer. She was definitely an attorney.

"Look," he said. "I'm the first to admit I lack parenting experience. And I'm going to need help. But I won't be treated like a criminal, either."

"I apologize. I was out of line."

He nodded. "Thank you for that."

"I really want for us to work together on what's best for Cody."

"Agreed."

"Good." She relaxed. "What if Cody and I come by—"

"I'd like for Cody to move in with me. Right away."

"What!" She stared at him as if he'd suggested she jump out of a plane without a parachute.

"I told you that first day, if he was my son, I'd do right by him. Well, I will. And for me, that means being a full-time father. Not pawning him off on his mother's relatives."

The plan that had started taking shape yesterday during Jacob's ride crystalized. He would be a better father than Oscar Burke and Brock Baron combined.

"I love Cody. You wouldn't be pawning him off on me."

"You'd be welcome to visit anytime. Your mother, too. Have him on weekends."

Mariana shook her head. "You can't possibly care for a toddler. You don't even have a crib."

"Small details that can be worked out."

"Have you ever bathed a child or changed a diaper?"

Diapers? Okay, he hadn't thought of that. "Larger details, but they can still be worked out. Other men manage to be fathers." He was thinking of Luke. "I'm sure I can learn, too."

"You work during the day. And you're gone every weekend to some rodeo."

"Cody's in day care now. There must be a suitable place between my house and the drill site."

She held up a hand as if to stop him. He almost expected her to say, "Your honor, I object."

What she did say was, "This is much, much too quick. He just lost Leah. He can't lose me, too. There has to be another solution."

"There is. You can move in with me, too."

"What!"

"Temporarily. Just until Cody adjusts. A month should be long enough, don't you think? Longer if necessary. I can get off work early on Thursday."

Her mouth worked, but no words came out.

Jacob couldn't help grinning. Seems he'd finally done it. Shocked the unflappable Mariana Snow into silence.

"Have you lost your mind?" Lucille Snow pressed her palms to her cheeks and squeezed her eyes shut. "You can't do this."

If Mariana had lost her mind, she wasn't the only one. Jacob was plumb crazy to suggest she stay with him. Then again, she'd agreed. What did that say about her?

"Mom, please. Don't make a big deal out of it."

"I'm going to lose my grandson."

"He'll be two hours away."

"What if he insists on full custody and

won't let me see Cody?" She bit out the word *he* as if Jacob were indeed the criminal he'd accused Mariana of calling him.

"He said you could visit as often as you wanted. Even have Cody for weekends. But if by some chance he refuses, we'll go after him. Grandparents have rights, too."

"You shouldn't have told him he was Cody's father."

"But he is Cody's father, and denying him his son would be wrong."

Last evening surely hadn't gone as planned. Mariana went from being the one in control to being a helpless bystander as Jacob made plans. If only she hadn't been so impulsive. She should have insisted they hammer out visitation before she introduced him to Cody.

"Leah wouldn't approve." Her mother's voice had started to shake. "I'd stop you if I could."

This…vehemence was new.

Mariana went over and put an arm around her mother's shoulders. "Working yourself up into a frenzy won't help."

"Cody's so little. He's already been uprooted once these past months." Her mother started to cry.

"Drive up again this weekend. Or maybe I'll

drive down. That way, Cody can see Grandma, too. She loves seeing him."

Mariana's grandmother was also in Austin. Though still living alone, she'd grown frailer this past year, ever since her hip replacement, and required more time and attention from her daughter.

"Watch him carefully." Mariana's mother brought her tears under control.

Him meaning Jacob. "I will, Mom. But he's not a brute. He was really pretty good with Cody the other day."

"He doesn't know the first thing about toddlers."

"Which is why I agreed to stay with him. Temporarily." And she wasn't leaving until he'd convinced her beyond a shadow of a doubt he was capable of parenting a small child for extended periods of time. It required more than a great dog, a nice yard and impressive cooking skills. "Leah trusted me to do what's best for Cody, and I think this is best."

She continued packing her suitcase, taking a mental inventory. Underwear. Toiletries. Four pairs of shoes. Workout clothes. Sleepwear.

Sleepwear? What should she bring? Mariana had never cohabitated with a man in a platonic relationship. She'd never cohabitated with a man period. Not that she was a prude. She'd spent nights at her boyfriend's place before. When she'd had a boyfriend. Sleepwear wasn't an issue then.

She settled on her two least-sexy pajamas and threw in a thick robe for good measure. Cody sometimes woke up during the night. She'd be appropriately covered should they find themselves wandering the house.

Helena, Mariana's secretary, had proved invaluable. She'd ordered a portable crib, a portable changing table, plastic crates to substitute for dresser drawers and all manner of small necessities. Then, she'd had the items delivered to Jacob's house. She'd also located a childproofing service. They were scheduled for later in the week.

Mariana saw no need to move Cody's furniture and belongings just yet. Best to wait and see how things progressed. Jacob might reconsider. His insistence on this arrangement was a knee-jerk reaction to her insistence that they wait.

And she'd only insisted because her mother had come unglued. Mariana's staying with Jacob seemed like a good compromise.

What had gone wrong the other day? she wondered. Mariana was usually good at coaxing people into doing what she wanted. It served her well in her profession. Yet she'd failed to coax Jacob into moving slowly. Was she blinded by his looks and appeal? She didn't want to label it attraction. She couldn't possibly be attracted to him. He wasn't at all the kind of guy she went for. Besides, he'd fathered her sister's child.

"Where's Cody?" Her mother peered down the hall, her expression anxious.

"In his room. Packing a suitcase."

"You're not leaving that up to him!" Her mother started for the door.

"Mom, come back. He's just playing."

To keep Cody occupied while she packed, Mariana had put a second suitcase on the floor of his room. That was all it took. Cody had spent the past twenty minutes filling the suitcase with mostly toys and picture books. She'd have to sneak in later when he wasn't looking and repack with clothes and shoes.

"How soon are you leaving?" Her mother's frown shouted her unhappiness.

"Soon. I promised Jacob we'd be there before dinner. We need to settle in before Cody's bedtime."

"Doesn't he rodeo every weekend?"

Would her mother *ever* call Jacob by his name?

"Yes, but he's planning on coming home early Sunday. To spend as much time as possible with Cody and get to know him."

Her mother harrumphed. "Your dad had every chance in the world to get to know you and your sister, and it didn't matter. He still chose rodeoing."

"Not every man is like Dad." Mariana picked through her jewelry box, selecting earrings and necklaces to take with her.

"You can't right his wrongs, you know." Her mother sniffed.

"What are you talking about?"

"Telling Cody's father about him. You think that Cody having a father in his life will make up for you and Leah missing out."

Mariana gaped at her mother. "That is so far from the truth."

"Is it?"

She couldn't possibly be trying to re-create the past by manipulating the present. Telling Jacob about his son was a matter of principle. Or wasn't it?

Leah had easily dismissed their father, content to live her life as if he never existed. Mariana had been different. She'd experienced an entire range of emotions where Zeb Snow was concerned. Anger at him for abandoning her, resentment that he wasn't there, longing to know him, hope that he'd change and come back for her.

No, Cody didn't deserve to grow up like either she or her sister had. Jacob Baron would be a good father. She had to believe that.

An hour later the three of them were loading the car, Cody again "helping." The Infiniti's small trunk and backseat were full to bursting.

"Have you got everything?" her mother asked. She'd already loaded her small suitcase into her car in preparation of returning to Austin.

Mariana wiped her forehead. "Probably not."

When they were finally ready to leave, her mother held Cody and cried as if he were leaving for a year.

"Mom, please. You're upsetting him."

Indeed, the boy had started whimpering. Though he could simply be tired. It was nap time.

Her mother straightened. "Call me when you get there."

"I will." Mariana lifted Cody and placed him in his car seat. His attention was immediately drawn to the boxes and bags piled on the seat beside him.

"My blanky." He slapped a plastic bag.

"That's right. It's your blanket." She thought he might sleep better with his own bedding.

"Bye, darling." Mariana's mother leaned into the car and kissed his forehead. "I love you."

"Bye-bye. Bye-bye." He waved out the window when Mariana shut the door.

Pivoting, she found herself engulfed in her mother's arms and the recipient of a hug as fierce as the one she'd given Cody.

"I hope you're not making a terrible mistake."

The statement, delivered in a foreboding tone, stayed with Mariana the entire drive to Jacob's house. She felt no better when she arrived and saw him standing outside, waiting.

Chapter 4

There was something surreal about sitting at the table with Jacob, lingering over breakfast while Cody played on the floor with Buster. They weren't a family, not in the traditional sense. Yet to anyone looking through the window, they could have passed for one.

"I'm glad all Cody's fussing didn't wake you," Mariana said, striving to keep her voice light and conversational.

Jacob unnerved her. His casual attire—T-shirt, jeans and bare feet—combined with his slightly tousled hair advertised just how recently he'd crawled out of bed—a bed located in the room across the hall from the one she and Cody occupied.

"He did wake me," Jacob said over the rim of his coffee mug.

"Oh. You didn't come out."

"I figured you'd have a harder time getting him back to sleep if Buster and I were there distracting him."

"You're probably right."

Mariana tugged self-consciously on the wrist of her long-sleeved jersey shirt. At home, she'd have stayed in her pajamas and robe until noon if the mood struck her. Here, she'd dressed in what amounted to workout clothes. Well, in her defense, she might push Cody around the block a few times in his stroller. It was good exercise.

"More toast?" Jacob held up a platter.

Mariana started to say no, then changed her mind. "Hate to see it go to waste." She snatched up the last piece.

Cinnamon toast. Prepared to perfection. She and Cody had both gobbled up an obscene amount, downing it with fresh-squeezed orange juice. Thank goodness her stay was temporary. Another month of meals like this one and the lasagna they had for dinner last night, and she wouldn't fit into her clothes.

"Have you always liked to cook?" she asked, resisting closing her eyes in ecstasy as she took another bite of toast.

"My mother taught me. She was quite accomplished in the kitchen. More home cooking than gourmet."

"I didn't realize."

"You're not alone. Most people took her for a socialite. Which she was. Being married to Brock calls for that. But she was a great mom, too."

"It was sad how she died. So unexpected."

"I'm not sure anyone ever gets over losing a loved one. You know that better than anyone."

"Yes, but we had time to prepare." Mariana absently twirled a spoon in her coffee. "A few months."

"Is it really better having time or not?" He looked away as if remembering. "I sometimes wonder what I'd have done differently if Mom had months to live rather than hours."

Such a serious conversation. Not at all what Mariana had intended when she inquired about his cooking abilities. But then, Jacob was apparently a lot deeper than she'd given him credit. Besides being intelligent and talented, he cooked, kept a semi-immaculate house, had a knack with animals and contemplated the meaning of life.

Hmm. Take away the rodeoing, and he'd be exactly the kind of man she'd always pictured herself with. Except, he did rodeo.

Which come to think of it, wasn't so terrible. His pastime provided a built-in safeguard to prevent her from losing her heart. With that stray lock of dark hair falling attractively over his brow, she was going to need every safeguard available.

"Varoom, varoom."

On the floor beside them, Cody made noises mimicking a roaring engine as he drove his toy truck up Buster's neck and between his ears. Mariana saved a piece of toast crust to slip to the dog later. He'd earned a reward for his boundless patience.

Her cell phone rang, calling to her from the guest bedroom down the hall.

"Excuse me." She started to rise, her glance darting nervously to Cody. "Can you watch him for a second?"

"Sure."

"If not, I'll—"

"I think I can manage to keep him out of

trouble for thirty seconds." He quirked one brow in amusement.

Good grief, he was handsome.

Pulling herself together, she dashed to the bedroom and grabbed her phone off the dresser. Her first instinct was to hurry back. She resisted, certain she'd look stupid and distrusting. The whole purpose of her staying here was to teach Jacob the skills he'd need to properly care for Cody.

Her boss's number appeared on the phone's display.

"Hi, Saul."

"We have a new client I want you to meet with tomorrow. 8:00 a.m. sharp."

It was just like him to get straight to the point. No greeting. No apologies for interrupting her scheduled day off. No inquiry as to how was she doing.

"Okay." She dug in her purse for the notebook she always kept there and a pen. "Shoot."

He recited a name, an address, cross streets and a phone number. "It's not far from your house."

Mariana didn't tell him she wasn't staying at her home these days. "Is she expecting me?"

"She *can't wait* to meet you."

Another client. With their cases making

the news on a regular basis, people Molinas had scammed were crawling out of the woodwork.

"All right," she said. "I'll check in with you when I get there."

Without so much as a simple "Thanks" or "Enjoy the rest of your day," Saul said goodbye and hung up.

She sighed. Her boss might not be the friendly, chatty type, but he had taught her a lot since she'd started working at Hasbrough and Colletti three years ago, and—this counted for a lot—he supported her bid for junior partner.

"Let me wash the dishes," she announced upon entering the dining area, only to come to a grinding halt, her breath trapped in her lungs.

Jacob sat with Cody on his lap. The instant her nephew spotted her, he erupted in a piercing wail.

She covered the distance in the span of a single heartbeat. "What happened?"

"He fell."

"How?"

"He tripped on the chair leg."

"You were supposed to be watching him." She reached for Cody, who held out his arms to her.

"I was. I watched him trip."

"Men," she huffed, cradling Cody's head and bouncing him on her hip.

"He's fine. Buster broke his fall. If anyone's hurt, it's him." Jacob stroked the dog's head. "I only looked away for a second."

She cut him some slack. Cody could move quickly. "It happens. I didn't mean to snap at you."

Cody abruptly let out a second wail and attempted to hurl himself from Mariana's grasp.

"What's wrong?" She glanced about and spotted the cause of his distress. "Buster has his truck."

The dog, oblivious to the drama surrounding him, had picked up the plastic dump truck and was carrying it away. Probably to his toy basket in the family room.

"Buster." That was all Jacob said. The dog turned immediately around. "Sit," he commanded and held his open palm beneath the dog's mouth. "Leave it."

The undamaged toy fell into Jacob's hand.

"Good boy." He rewarded the dog with another petting.

Cody squealed with delight, fighting harder than before to get down.

Mariana deposited him on the floor, and he scurried over to Buster.

"Again," the boy demanded, all smiles.

So much for worrying about his precious toy.

"You try." Jacob gave the truck to Cody, who shoved it at Buster's mouth. "Easy now," Jacob coaxed. Once Buster had the toy, Jacob told Cody, "Say, leave it."

"Weave it," Cody commanded and broke into giggles when Buster obediently relinquished the toy.

Okay, another crisis averted, Mariana thought. And Jacob had somewhat redeemed himself. But what would he do when Buster wasn't around?

They wound up washing the dishes together. Another surreal experience. The last man Mariana had performed domestic chores with was her boyfriend. Her long-ago boyfriend.

Deprivation. That must explain her interest in Jacob. She refused to use the words *attraction* or *fascination*.

"What time are you getting up in the morning?" she asked, carting another stack of dishes from the table to the sink. She'd deposited Cody in front of the TV and put his favorite "learning animal names" DVD in the player to watch.

"Five."

"That's early. I thought the rodeo was in Allen." A ninety-minute drive at most.

"I have chores to do first, then I'm meeting Daniel at the Roughneck."

"Good luck."

"I'll leave some coffee in the pot."

He smiled, and her heart did that silly little lurch again. She waited until she could trust her voice. "I have an eight o'clock appointment myself. Cody and I will be out of here by seven."

"I'll give you a spare house key and the code for the alarm system."

"Thanks." She'd thought about a key but hadn't felt comfortable asking.

"Was that a work call you got earlier? I wasn't being nosy," he added quickly. "More curious. What do you do at Hasbrough and Colletti?" Rinsing coffee mugs beneath the running faucet, he loaded them into the dishwasher. "Bail celebrities out of trouble?"

His last remark was delivered with a chuckle, so she didn't take offense. Not that she would. Any number of celebrities, politicians and prominent local citizens had programmed Hasbrough and Colletti's number into their phone's speed dial. Without question, they were the top fix-it law firm in the Dallas area, if not the state.

When a starlet was busted on her second DUI, Hasbrough and Colletti hurriedly had her admitted into an ultra-private rehab facility, then kept her face out of the papers as much as possible. When a congressman was caught red-handed texting explicit messages and selfies to a woman not his wife, they suppressed the scandal, wrote carefully worded press releases and repaired his flailing career.

It wasn't, however, all they did. Hasbrough and Colletti's more humanitarian cases were what drew Mariana to them in the first place and the reason she strived to build her career there.

"Actually, I'm one of the attorneys handling a dozen joint suits against Medallion Investments."

Jacob whistled. "No fooling."

"You've heard?"

"Who hasn't? Paulo Molinas supposedly scammed hundreds of people out of their life savings with some kind of Ponzi scheme."

"There's no supposedly about it." Mariana's chest tightened. It always did when she thought about the losses their clients had suffered. Senior citizens on fixed incomes. Single moms struggling to provide their children with a college education. Widows and widowers losing their inheritances. All of them robbed. "He's a thief. And we're not only going to prove it, we're going to obtain as much money as possible for our clients."

Jacob paused and studied her with interest. "You like your job."

"I *love* my job. This is one field of law where I can really do some good. I'm hoping to make junior partner. I'm on the short list. Depending on how this case goes, I could be a shoo-in."

"Passion and ambition. I respect that in a person."

"Because you love what you do, too?"

"Because of what I hope to accomplish."

"Which is?"

"Alternative energy. My goal is to form a new division at Baron Energies."

Now it was her turn to whistle. "I'm impressed."

Who knew? She and Jacob shared something. Passion and ambition for their jobs. She felt her interest in him growing and attempted to curb it. Standing hip to hip at the sink, discussing topics that moved and inspired them as his dark eyes roved her face with unmasked interest, made the task downright impossible.

"What are your plans for the rest of the day?" Mariana asked, wiping down the counter. It was one topic they hadn't covered.

"Move furniture. Make closet space for you. Get ready for the weekend. Later there's a family dinner at the Roughneck."

"On a Thursday?"

"New baby in the family. Even more reason for a get-together. My sisters and their families will be there. Carly's future stepdaughter is about Cody's age. Daniel, too."

"What about your father?"

"Count on it," Jacob said. "His wife, Julieta, too, and her son, Alex. He's five."

"Sounds nice." With an evening to herself, Mariana could prepare for her meeting tomorrow morning while Cody slept.

"I'd like to take Cody with me. Introduce him to the family."

Her hand stilled. She should have seen this coming. Automatically, her glance strayed to the family room where Cody played happily. "Isn't it a little soon? Maybe you should wait until the test results are back."

"Brock isn't only my father, he's my boss. Having a son can impact my job, and he has a right to be told."

There was logic to Jacob's argument. Not enough, however, to convince Mariana he was ready to fly solo. "How about we have a few lessons first? You haven't even changed a diaper yet."

"I have a better idea. Why don't you come with us?"

"What! No, I don't think so."

"Why not?"

"Because your family will wonder about us. You and I. How will you explain our... relationship?"

He shrugged. "My son's aunt."

To her chagrin, her cheeks warmed. "They'll jump to conclusions."

"I'll say we met through work."

"They'll still jump to conclusions."

"I think they'll figure out pretty quickly there's nothing going on."

Did he really not feel the sparks flying between them? Mariana didn't know whether to be relieved or insulted.

She raised her chin a notch and chose the lesser of two evils. "What time are we leaving?"

"Around four-thirty."

"I'll pack Cody's diaper bag and give him a bath."

"I'll help."

"That's not necessary."

"As you said, I need lessons." His earlier smile returned, which he showered on her.

The warmth in her cheeks spread—all the way to her toes. She fought it. He may not be having any romantic inclinations, but the same couldn't be said for her.

There was usually a certain amount of underlying tension when Jacob visited his family. Today, nerves were added to the mix.

He vowed to steer clear of any alternative energy discussions. No extolling the benefits. No mentioning of Starr Solar Systems' potential sale. No saying things like, "If we're not moving forward, we're moving backward."

Today, he was introducing Cody to his family. Whether he told them Mariana and Cody were living with him depended on how things went.

"Pretty spectacular." Mariana had her nose practically pressed against the passenger-side window.

The Roughneck Ranch could be impressive to newcomers, Jacob had to admit. While not the largest or the fanciest spread by any means, the vast grounds were meticulously maintained, the peach orchard lush in the growing season, the horse barn and arena state-of-the-art, and the sprawling country-style house charming.

He pulled into the driveway, wide enough to accommodate four vehicles abreast, and took stock of who else was here. As predicted, Luke and Carly had already arrived, which meant Cody would have Luke's daughter, Rosie, for a playmate. Also Lizzie, Christopher and the new baby. Daniel, too. Evidently Savannah and Travis were either late or not coming.

"I firsty." Cody, securely buckled into his car seat, kicked his feet as if running.

"I'll get him," Jacob said when Mariana climbed out of the truck and started toward the rear passenger door.

"Okay." She took a step back and waited, giving him an opportunity for another of those child care lessons.

Reaching the passenger side rear door, he maneuvered around her. The scent of what-ever it was she wore, lotion, body wash, cologne, reached him and tantalized him. Citrus, he thought. Discernible but not over-powering, and very sexy.

So were the clothes. Sexy, that was. He liked her in skirts. The jeans she'd chosen weren't bad either, and fit her like a glove. She'd paired them with another set of ridiculously high heels. He had to admit, the look suited her. Another time, under different circumstances...

Bending over Cody, he unfastened the many buckles. Forget being in a hurry.

"Where Buster?" Cody asked.

"He's at home, buddy."

"I want Buster."

"Later, okay?" He lifted Cody out of the seat and held him against his chest as he'd seen Mariana do.

Cody made whimpering sounds. "Firsty."

"He didn't sleep well last night." Mariana reached over and smoothed his hair. "Or nap much earlier. I hope he doesn't throw a fit while we're here."

"We can leave early if that happens."

She'd explained all about the terrible twos on their drive over. From her description, Jacob decided that was one aspect of parenting he could do without.

"I hate to disrupt your family dinner."

She was nervous, too. He could tell by the

way she kept tugging on the sleeves of her blazer and the strained quality of her voice.

"We'll be fine," he insisted, though he wasn't entirely sure.

They started up the shrub-lined walkway to the front door. On impulse, Jacob placed a hand on the center of her back, his touch light but, he hoped, reassuring.

The zing was instantaneous. She tensed, but he didn't remove his hand. Not until they were at the door. The sensation coursing through his fingers was much too enjoyable. Too addictive.

He told himself this fascination with Mariana was a fluke. That she was simply a novelty, someone very different from the typical woman he dated. *When* he dated. These past nine months his work and rodeo schedule had left little time for any social life. Which must account for his preoccupation. It had been too long since Jacob had placed his hand on a woman's back.

"Hey! You're here." Carly rushed forward to welcome them.

During family dinners and holidays, the kitchen and adjoining great room were the central meeting places. She'd obviously been helping Julieta with the cooking, judging by the hot pads she quickly tucked between her arm and side.

"Sorry we're late," Jacob said, giving her a brief hug and peck on the cheek.

While not exactly bosom buddies, he and Carly had grown closer since she and Luke became engaged. Same with Lizzie, though for a different reasons. She'd been his supporter from the beginning, backing his proposals to Brock and championing his bid for more responsibility.

Would she resent him now that he had the first Baron grandchild, usurping her daughter? Jacob didn't think so. Then again, she could see Jacob's fatherhood as a threat to her position in the family hierarchy.

"Are you going to introduce us?" Carly asked, her eyes landing on Mariana and snapping with curiosity.

Luke must not have told her anything, which Jacob appreciated.

"This is Mariana Snow." He put his hand on the center of her back again and was rewarded with another zing. With his other arm, he bounced Cody. "And her nephew, Cody."

"Nice to meet you, Mariana." Carly clasped both of Mariana's hands in hers, brows raised in an I-wonder-what's-going-on-here arch.

Then, she turned to Cody. "How do you do, young man?"

He stared at Carly, then blinked, obviously not sure how to respond.

She held out her hand to him. "I'm Carly."

Instead of shaking her hand, he slapped her palm.

"Okay." Carly's smile increased.

"He wants to give you a high five," Mariana explained.

"Oh! I get it." Carly held up her palm, and Cody slapped it.

"Hi, hi!"

"Hi to you, too."

He twisted in Jacob's arms, arching his back to look at Mariana. "Mama, Mama."

"It's okay, honey," she said.

Carly appeared confused. "I thought you said he was your nephew."

"He is." To her credit, Mariana didn't fluster. "My sister passed away a few months ago. Cody has been living with me since, and he sometimes gets confused."

Carly's features fell. "I'm so sorry."

"Thank you."

To avoid any prolonged awkwardness, Jacob crossed the entry to the great room.

"How did you and Jacob meet?" Carly

walked beside them, making casual conversation.

Mariana inhaled sharply. As she'd predicted, Carly assumed she and Jacob were dating.

"At the Louisiana State Fair Rodeo," he said. It wasn't a lie. The rodeo was where he'd first met Mariana.

"I should've guessed." Carly laughed, then instantly sobered. "I didn't mean that how it sounded," she said to Mariana. "Jacob doesn't pick up women at rodeos. It's just that rodeoing is all he does besides work." She groaned in despair. "I'm making this worse. Ignore me. Please."

Jacob and Mariana exchanged a look. He smiled. She didn't.

"Who's this?"

The booming voice belonged to Brock and came from where he sat on the large sectional, his injured leg propped up on a footrest, the crutches he still used beside him.

"Brace yourself," Jacob murmured to Mariana. Aloud, he said, "This is Mariana and Cody."

Luke was the first to come over, and he brought his daughter Rosie with him, holding her by the hand. Jacob set Cody on his feet, crossing his fingers that the two toddlers would become fast friends.

They took a moment to size each other up. Then, Cody abruptly spun and clutched Mariana's leg as he had the day he'd met Jacob. For reasons not exactly clear, Rosie began to cry.

"Give them time," Luke said matter-of-factly.

Not exactly the auspicious beginning Jacob had hoped for. It only went downhill from there.

"We're having a fall carnival at the store this weekend," Carly said. "You should come. Bring Cody and Mariana."

"We'll see."

"Aren't you competing in the Texas Stampede this weekend?" Brock said from where he sat on the large sectional.

"I'm coming back early." Jacob didn't go into details.

"Is that wise?"

"I only need to place twice more in bull riding to qualify. Three times in bronc riding." There were a good three rodeos left. Four if push came to shove and he was willing to travel halfway across the country.

Brock grunted with satisfaction. Or dissatisfaction. It was hard to tell.

"Not now, Dad," Carly admonished.

"He doesn't want to lose steam this late in the race."

Carly rolled her eyes at Jacob, then latched on to Mariana's arm. "I promise to take good care of her and Cody. You hang with the guys."

"Maybe I should—"

"It's all right. Come see the baby," she told Mariana and promptly whisked her into the kitchen.

With no other choice, Jacob wandered into the great room where Brock, Christopher and Daniel were watching a football game on the large-screen TV.

Daniel aimed the remote at the TV and lowered the volume on the football game. "Hey, how's it going?"

"Can't complain."

"You look tired."

He was. Like Cody, he hadn't slept much last night. There were two strangers in his house. One who'd kept him awake with his crying and one who'd kept him awake with thoughts he really shouldn't be having. Jacob's life was already complicated enough.

"Been a long week." He lowered himself onto an empty cushion near Daniel rather than

Brock. He hoped the distance would discourage conversation about Mariana and Cody. It didn't.

"What's this about coming home early on Sunday?"

Daniel would pick now to ask Jacob about that. "I'll tell you later."

Brock tipped his head in the direction of the kitchen. "How long you been seeing that sweet young thing?"

"We're just friends."

Jacob's reply was met with a loud, raucous chuckle from Brock. "She doesn't look like the friend type."

Daniel shrugged in agreement. Christopher was no help, either.

"Her sister died a few months ago, which is why she has guardianship of Cody. I'm…" Jacob paused. "Helping. It hasn't been easy for them."

"That's a shame. For sure." Brock's gaze landed on Jacob and intensified. "Doesn't explain why you brought her here."

"I can't bring a friend to dinner?"

"'Course you can. Just that now isn't the best time for you to get involved with someone. Got a lot on your plate, and a lot riding on going to Nationals."

Jacob ground his teeth together rather than say what he was thinking—that Brock had no business dictating his personal life.

Luckily, he was spared a further lecture when Julieta entered the room brandishing a large tray with corn chips and her specialty: homemade *pico de gallo.*

"Who's hungry?" She set the tray down on the large knotty pine coffee table. Her five-year-old son Alex tumbled in after her, barely giving her time to steady the tray before digging in.

"Hi, Jacob," the boy said, shoveling a dripping chip into his mouth.

"Hi, yourself." Jacob smiled back, looking at Alex with a new perspective.

Brock had also adopted Alex, making the boy Jacob's brother, as well. Did Brock treat Alex differently than he had Jacob and Daniel? Unlike them, Alex had lived under Brock's roof since he was a baby.

Julieta plunked down between Alex and Brock. "I like your girlfriend."

"We're not seeing each other." How many times was Jacob going to have to explain himself?

She winked playfully. "Well, maybe you should start."

"I vote yes," Daniel concurred.

"No, he shouldn't," Brock insisted, leaning forward and reaching for another serving of chips.

"Oh, you." Julieta leaned over and pressed an affectionate kiss to his cheek.

Jacob's emotions battled as he watched the two of them. It was evident they cared for each other. Also evident they were well matched. Julieta didn't take any guff from Brock. She also worked hard for Baron Energies as head of public relations.

The complete opposite of Jacob's soft-spoken and quiet-mannered mother, who'd concentrated her efforts on making the best home for her husband and their children. It still pained Jacob when he saw Julieta with Brock. They might be well matched, but if his mother hadn't died, she'd be here now, and he would have no reservations about introducing Cody.

One of the Dallas Cowboys players made a touchdown, and attention was refocused on the TV, for which Jacob was grateful. Julieta left. Thirty minutes later, she returned, announcing that dinner was ready. Everyone wound their way to the long dining table at the other end of the great room. Lizzie brought the baby along in one of those carrying contraptions and set her in the corner near her seat.

"I'll get the high chair from the truck," Jacob said upon seeing Mariana. She and Carly had just returned from outside where the youngsters had been playing.

"Thanks." She smiled, looking a little worn for the worse but holding her own. His sisters must not have been too tough on her.

"Don't bother," Julieta said, stopping Jacob. "I thought Rosie and Cody could sit at the play table today."

Luke was setting up a child-size table and four chairs in the kitchen. He must have brought it from home because Rosie was staking claim to it. She clearly didn't appreciate Cody's interest.

"Will they be okay alone?" Mariana gazed worriedly at the kitchen.

"I'll sit with them," Alex offered and started off.

Wasn't that a little like having a fox guard the henhouse?

"I don't know...." Jacob frowned.

"They'll be fine," Julieta insisted.

He looked to Luke and Carly.

"She's right, they'll be fine." His friend didn't appear concerned.

To the children's credit, they behaved well. For the first ten minutes. Long enough for everyone at the adult table to be served. Then, all hell broke loose. A small commotion ensued, accompanied by a high-pitched scream and then outraged crying.

"It's okay," Alex called from the kitchen. "Cody just spilled his milk on Rosie."

By then, Jacob, Mariana, Luke and Carly were all standing.

"Excuse me," Mariana said. "I'll be right back."

"Wait for me." Jacob went after her.

The next moment, Cody came running full tilt around the corner, his face a mask of unhappiness and tears streaming down his cheeks.

Jacob was closer and scooped him up. "It's okay, buddy."

Cody buried his face in Jacob's shoulder.

"Is he hurt?" Mariana hurried over.

"I don't think so."

By then, Luke had retrieved Rosie, who was also in tears.

"We can get you more milk." Mariana soothed Cody by rubbing his back.

"Wanna go home." Cody hiccuped and buried his face in Jacob's shirt. "Peese, Daddy."

The room went silent except for a small gasp from Lizzie. Jacob felt more than saw the stares. This wasn't how he'd intended to break the news.

Brock's hand came down on the table. "What's going on here? Why did he call you Daddy?"

"He's just confused," Carly offered. "He calls Mariana Mama."

"Don't you think you should unconfuse him?"

Jacob felt a sudden flood of emotions, the strongest one a need to protect and defend this small child who, until only last week, hadn't had a father in his life. Jacob might not be much of one yet, but there was no time like the present to start.

"He's calling me Daddy because he's my son."

Julieta dropped her fork, which clattered to the table. Daniel cleared his throat and looked uncomfortable. Carly murmured, "I knew it!"

Brock recovered quickly. "Your son?"

"Before you ask, I only just found out." Jacob touched Mariana's arm and nodded at the table, indicating for her to take her chair.

She did but squirmed uncomfortably as if the seat were made of thorns. He also sat, balancing Cody in his lap. "Cody's moved in with me."

Everyone started talking, slowly at first, then all at once. Jacob answered questions as best he could, until one from Brock silenced everyone at the table.

"How do you expect to work *and* rodeo with a boy to take care of?"

"I'll manage. One way or the other."

"You need to qualify for Nationals."

"And I will."

"Maybe you should let his aunt keep him until then." Brock cut into a thick slab of pork roast. "Be easier on everyone."

"Cody's my son, and he's staying with me."

"Seems you've made your bed, you can sleep in it. Don't expect any special consideration from me."

Anger gathered inside Jacob. He shoved it aside. This wasn't the time or place to start an argument. "Trust me, I don't."

They left soon after dinner, citing that Cody's bedtime was fast approaching. Jacob was also tired, and it had nothing to do with the need for sleep.

What had he been thinking earlier? Brock

hadn't changed and never would. Cody was no more a grandson to him than Jacob was a son. Hoping for anything different was a complete and utter waste of time.

Chapter 5

Mariana stood at the French doors, watching Jacob play with Cody in the backyard. More accurately, she watched Jacob watching Cody play by himself. The two weren't exactly interacting. It was, however, a start. Jacob sat on a lawn chair and kept an eye on Cody, who crawled on his hands and knees, pushing his truck in circles.

She hadn't objected when Jacob suggested he take Cody out to play. For one, she'd needed to organize her notes for a client meeting in the morning. For another, he'd been gone since Friday and only recently returned from the rodeo in Allen.

They'd hardly spoken at all about the fiasco of a dinner at the Roughneck. Jacob assured her not to worry. Right.

Mariana continued studying him through the door's small windowpanes. She gave Jacob credit for maintaining his cool under what had to have been intense pressure from his family. After saying their goodbyes, some terse, others warm, they'd left the ranch. Jacob's brother Daniel had called on the drive home. Their conversation was short and unrevealing, and ended with Jacob promising to see him in the morning.

Mariana gave Jacob his space, both before he left for the rodeo and since his return. As much as she might want to, it wasn't her place to interfere in his family matters. Not unless Cody was directly and negatively affected. That didn't stop her from being curious, which is why she stood at the door, staring.

"Enough," she told herself and turned away. Cody was fine, Jacob deserved his privacy and she had plenty of work waiting for her. She returned to the dining table where she'd set up her laptop. At home, she had a small office. Here, she was forced to make do with what was available.

To her surprise, she lost herself in her

work for—she glanced at the clock on her laptop—thirty-seven minutes. Really? She hadn't worked more than ten minutes straight through since taking over Cody's care.

She went to the door, telling herself she was being overprotective—then telling herself she wasn't protective enough when Jacob and Cody were nowhere to be seen. Alarm coursing through her, she grabbed her coat, pushed open the door and rushed outside.

"Jacob!" she hollered. "Cody!"

"Here." The reply came from the paddock and stalls.

She raced there, only to come to a grinding halt. Jacob was riding Amigo, and he had Cody sitting in the saddle with him!

"What are you doing?" she demanded, on the move again. She stopped when she reached the paddock, considering for just a moment the wisdom of climbing through the rails.

"I'd say riding but we're just walking."

Jacob wore a smile, his first of the evening. So did Cody. His reached from ear to ear, and his small hands waved excitedly.

"Horsey," he exclaimed. "I widing."

"Oh, my God." Mariana's heart pounded. "He's not holding on."

"I've got him," Jacob assured her.

Indeed, his left arm was wrapped securely around Cody's middle as they walked the perimeter of the lighted paddock. Buster followed behind, tail wagging.

"He could fall," Mariana protested.

"We couldn't be going any slower."

Okay, they were progressing at a snail's pace. And the paddock wasn't large, maybe fifty by fifty feet. Also, the horse visibly limped from the bad hips Jacob had mentioned.

Mariana chewed her bottom lip. After another two loops around the paddock, she began to relax. Marginally. Cody called out, "Hi, hi," with each pass they made, his little stocking cap sitting askew on his head.

All right. The two of them were cute together. If she'd brought her phone with her, she'd have snapped a picture.

On the next loop, Jacob pulled the horse to a stop in front of her. "You want to give it a try?"

"What? Are you kidding?"

"You have ridden before?"

"Not for years and not often. Leah was the equestrian in our family. Well, she and my dad."

Jacob dismounted and reached for Cody. When the boy started to cry, Jacob left him in the saddle.

"Will he be all right like that?" Mariana bent and slid between the rails to stand in the paddock.

"I won't let anything happen. I promise." There was a strength in his tone that was surprisingly reassuring. Adding to that, Amigo had dropped his head and didn't appear to be going anywhere. "I've met him, you know," Jacob said.

"My dad?" She emerged on the other side of the fence. Amigo didn't move, even when she walked around him to join Jacob. "I'd be surprised if you hadn't met him at some point. He's been involved in rodeo one way or the other for thirtysomething years."

"Are you two close?"

"Hardly," she scoffed. "I can count on one hand the number of times I've seen him in the past ten years."

"I'm sorry."

"Yeah, well, these things happen." She suppressed the unhappy feelings that always accompanied any discussion of her father and forced a lightness into her voice. "It's probably for the best."

"Was Leah close to him?"

"She saw him more, being a competitive barrel racer and all. But they weren't close either."

"Does he know about Cody?"

Her stomach tightened. Couldn't they talk about something else besides her father? "He made a token appearance when Cody was born. That was the last any of us has seen him. He didn't even show up at Leah's memorial service."

"Guilt can cause people to do things they regret."

"Hmm." She hadn't thought that guilt might be what kept her father away. Did he regret his treatment of his family? "It makes no difference."

"Are you sure?"

She reached up and patted Cody's leg, the wall of anger she'd built and fortified through the years cracking ever so slightly. What she'd give for him not to suffer the same affliction as her and her sister. It was why she'd told Jacob about his son.

Please, please, be a better man than my father. She was risking so much. Cody's entire future.

"Care to take a spin?" Jacob nodded at the horse.

This wasn't the change of subject she'd been hoping for. "No way." She laughed.

"If it makes you feel better, I'll lead Amigo. Cody will love it," he added as further incentive.

"We could both fall."

"I'll catch you."

His eyes lingered on her face, and she swore he moved ever so slightly closer to her. Or was it she who leaned into him, drawn by an invisible and irresistible pull?

Next thing she knew, he was helping her mount, lifting Cody and fitting him snugly between her and the saddle horn. Amigo, good horse that he was, stood perfectly still.

"Ready?"

Oh, brother. She locked Cody to her with her left arm. With her right hand, she gripped the saddle horn for dear life. "I guess."

Jacob led the horse at an even slower walk, if that was possible. Cody squealed with delight, pointing at this and that and babbling. When Jacob started talking, Cody quieted as if listening. Mariana listened, too. She hung on every word.

"I'm sorry about the other day," he said. "My family is complicated."

"Trust me, if there's one thing I get, it's complicated family dynamics."

"Brock and I don't always see eye to eye." Jacob gazed at the horizon as he talked, though she suspected he was seeing something different in his mind.

"Parents and children often don't."

"He's my adoptive father. My real father's in prison."

She knew that but didn't say so. Jacob might not appreciate that she'd run a background check on him before approaching him about Cody. Because she was a big believer that children weren't defined by their parents' mistakes—she herself was a prime example—she didn't count it against Jacob.

"If my mother could arrange it," she said, "my father would be in prison, too. Not that he's committed a felony," she amended, then could have bitten her tongue. Jacob must hate being reminded of his father's crimes. "Sorry. I didn't—"

"It's all right. My dad made his choices."

And they had been bad ones. Mariana had learned a lot researching Oscar Burke. He'd not only embezzled two million from the financial firm where he'd worked and taken that money out of the country, he'd committed fraud and tax evasion. If that weren't enough, he'd run off with another woman, a coworker at the firm. In prison, he'd participated in an attack on a guard, compounding his crimes and lengthening his stay.

Poor Peggy. Jacob's mom had suffered a very public, very messy scandal that ended in divorce. Until then, the Burkes had been prominent citizens in the Houston area with not even their closest friends and relatives having any idea of Oscar Burke's clandestine activities. Peggy moved her two young boys twice to escape the gossip, finally settling in Dallas. There, she met Brock and remarried and had what appeared to be a mostly satisfying life.

Maybe not so much for Jacob.

"Brock adopted me and Daniel when I was nine. I think both he and my mom thought a new last name would stop the kids at school from picking on us."

The rocking motion of the horse seemed to have quieted Cody. It was causing Mariana's limbs to relax, too. Who'd have thought she'd feel this comfortable on a horse? With Cody, no less.

"Did it?" she mused aloud.

"After the third school, yeah. I had communications problems with some of the other boys. When they teased me and Daniel, I tended to communicate with my fists."

"Oh, my."

"I stopped fighting eventually. Things got a little better, but we weren't one big happy family by any means. I think my mother expected Brock to be the kind of father she desperately wanted for her sons. He was decent to me and Daniel, don't get me wrong. But he always loved his own children to a fault. In his defense, it was unfair of my mom or Daniel and me to expect anything else."

That might explain why Jacob was a senior safety manager at a drill site rather than an executive in the corporate headquarters. Then again, Mariana wasn't one to judge. Her own father fell so short of the mark, it wasn't funny.

"Brock cares about you, even if he comes on strong," she said. "I could see it."

"I know he does." Jacob patted the side of Amigo's neck as they made another round of the paddock. "He's actually taken what I guess you'd call an interest in me a few times. When I was high school, I started playing sports and rodeoing. Jet was still too young for both. Brock came to every one of my games and every one of my rodeos. It helped that Carly was competing in barrel racing at the same time. All good things come to an end, however. I went off to college and by then Jet was old enough to start competing."

"I'm sure Brock's just as proud of your academic and business accomplishments."

"He isn't. He respects them for sure. Buckles and trophies are what impress him."

How much, she wondered, did that have to do with his current race for a national championship title?

"Carly and Leah were acquainted," he said. "Friendly rivals apparently. Leah told me that."

"I didn't realize." Interesting, Mariana thought. That might explain how Leah had come to choose Jacob for Cody's father. "Small world" was her only comment.

He came to a stop by the gate. "Another round?"

"I think we're about done." Mariana glanced down at Cody. If they continued riding, he might fall asleep again and wind up being awake half the night. She had an early morning tomorrow and couldn't afford to be dragging her feet.

Jacob helped her down first, then he handed her Cody. "I'll unsaddle Amigo and put him up."

"All right." She found herself looking into Jacob's face, which was only inches from hers, and searching for any visible scars of his youthful ordeals. There were none. All his wounds must have been on the inside. "I still can't believe I rode a horse with Cody," she said with a smile.

Before she quite knew what was happening, Jacob leaned down and brushed his lips across hers.

The kiss wasn't long. Quite short, in fact. Just a soft, light whisper of a caress. She couldn't call it chaste, however. At least, her reaction wasn't chaste. A wave of heat washed over her from head to toe, leaving her breathless and a little disconcerted.

She drew back first. "I, ah, we can't..."

He increased the space between them by taking a step back. "You're right. I don't know what came over me. Sorry."

"It's been a strange few days. None of us is ourselves."

"Forget it happened."

"I'll see you inside." She headed toward the gate, her legs unsteady, Cody pressed close to her body as if he could shield her from her soaring emotions.

Jacob had kissed her!

And while she hadn't exactly kissed him back, it was still wrong. And foolish. She couldn't afford to get hurt, and any involvement with him was just asking for it. Look at her parents. She more than anyone knew rodeo cowboys weren't the best husband material.

More important, she had Cody to look out for. His future was depending on this adjustment period. She couldn't afford to make any mistakes.

Jacob was right. She needed to forget the kiss happened.

She got as far as the family room before stopping and touching her lips with the tips of her fingers.

Daniel called Jacob as he was heading home from work, wanting to finalize their plans to attend the Lucky Draw Rodeo in Round Rock. Since they were driving rather than flying, they'd have to leave bright and early Friday morning in order to make it in time for the afternoon events.

Jet wouldn't be going, his interest in rodoe-

ing dimming in recent weeks. Understand-
able. His fiancée and future stepdaughters
were more important.

"What are you going to do about the kid?"
Daniel asked after they'd hammered out a few
details. By kid, he meant Cody.

Jacob sat at a light, combing his fingers
through his disarrayed hair. He was almost
home, having left work after a grueling
eleven-hour shift. He'd checked with Mariana right before his brother called. She was
picking up Cody from day care and would be
home when he arrived.

"I'm not sure." Jacob had been wondering
the same thing himself all day.

"Can't his aunt take care of him?"

Daniel had been shocked when Jacob broke
the news at dinner last week. Hadn't everyone? Then he'd congratulated Jacob. The only
one who did. It was when Jacob started talking about Cody and the family's reaction that
Daniel clammed up. Jacob didn't make a big
deal of it. Daniel had his own issues with the
Barons. The two brothers always had that in
common.

"She could, I guess," he answered slowly.

"Then what's the problem?"

"Cody's my son. My responsibility. Expecting Mariana to watch him while I'm out of town isn't fair. Especially since this may not be the last weekend."

"She has guardianship of him."

"I'm asking for full custody."

"Really? When did you decide that?"

"You sound like you disapprove."

There was a pause before Daniel answered. "It's a big step. How does Mariana feel?"

"She's cooperating."

He and his "housemate" were walking on tiptoes around each other the past few days. He had only himself to blame for that. What had he been thinking, kissing her like that?

He'd been thinking how pretty she looked. How easy and natural it was talking to her. How it should be against the law for a woman to smell as good as she did.

Contemplating any kind of relationship other than platonic was a waste of time and energy. They couldn't be more ill-suited for each other, and the timing couldn't be worse. And yet the kiss had set off a chain reaction inside him. Interest built swiftly to attraction, attraction to desire. All from a kiss that was hardly more than peck.

In hindsight, having her live with him may not have been his most brilliant idea. The temptation to taste those lips again would be hard to resist.

"So take him with us."

Jacob blinked himself back to the present and the conversation with his brother.

"I can't bring a two-year-old to a rodeo. Not without a babysitter."

"Ask his aunt."

Jacob started to object, then reconsidered. Would she go? Probably not. "She isn't a fan of rodeos."

"Don't know unless you ask."

He could. What was the worst that could happen? She'd say no, then he'd see if she wouldn't mind watching Cody for the weekend.

Except what message would that be sending? He was the one who'd insisted on his ability to handle parenthood. Were there reputable babysitting services in Round Rock? There had to be. But Mariana wouldn't like that, either.

"I'll figure something out," he said. "If I don't talk to you before then, see you Friday morning."

Mariana's car was in the driveway when Jacob pulled in a few minutes later, the rear passenger door wide-open. She must have had her arms full and forgotten to close it. He came back after parking his truck in the garage and shut the car door. Entering the house through the garage, he was immediately accosted by Buster.

"Missed you, too, pal." He gave the excited dog a petting before proceeding to the kitchen, where he was accosted again. This time by the aroma of dinner. Mariana stood at the counter, removing plates from the cupboard. Cody played on the floor at her feet, an array of pots and their lids surrounding him. He was enthralled, moving lids from one pan to the other. "You cooked?" Jacob asked.

"I stopped for Chinese takeout on the way home. Is that okay?"

"Great. I love Chinese food."

"I feel bad. You've been doing all the cooking."

While she set the cartons on the table, Jacob grabbed Cody and placed him in the high chair. Cody squealed his objection until Mariana set a bowl of lo mein in front of him. Ignoring the fork she gave him, he dug in with both hands.

While they ate, Mariana discussed her day and the progress she was making on the Paulo

Molinas case. Their first settlement offer had been flatly rejected by her clients.

"Does he have the money to settle?" Jacob listened with only one ear. He was too busy thinking of how to broach the topic of the rodeo with her.

"Absolutely. His attorneys are claiming he doesn't, which is a lie. Our team is still uncovering accounts he's hidden. And there's always the insurance. Medallion Investments carried a large policy."

Hidden accounts made Jacob think of his own father, a place he'd rather not go. Not today.

"What are your plans for the weekend?" he abruptly asked.

"I was hoping my mom would come for a visit, but Grandma caught a cold and isn't feeling well." Disappointment tinged Mariana's voice. "Mom thinks she should stay in case Grandma gets worse."

An idea sprang suddenly to mind. How far was Round Rock from where her mother lived? Jacob did a quick mental calculation. Forty-five minutes at most. Was it feasible?

"Daniel and I are competing at the Lucky Draw Rodeo this weekend."

"Ah." Her monosyllabic reply couldn't be less enthusiastic.

"I was thinking, it's not far from where your mom lives. Why don't you and Cody ride with us? We could drop you off and pick you up Sunday evening after the rodeo."

She deliberated for all of one second. "No."

"Why not?"

"A road trip with a two-year-old is no fun."

"We're talking a few hours. He'll sleep for half of that."

"I have work to do."

"Take it with you. What's the difference if you do it here or at your mom's?" His argument must have made some sense for she appeared to waver.

"I don't know...."

"Your mom will really appreciate it."

She studied him from across the table, her chopsticks poised above her plate. "This *arrangement* is much more to your advantage than mine."

Busted.

He dived into his Mongolian beef with a fork, having never mastered the art of eating with chopsticks. "I prefer to think of it as a compromise. And your mother does get to see her grandson."

Mariana absently sopped up the grape juice Cody had spilled with a paper napkin before he could smear it around the high chair tray. "Maybe."

"We leave Friday morning."

"I have to work on Friday."

"Then meet us in Round Rock Friday evening, grab Cody and head to Austin."

"Wait a minute!" She laid her chopsticks aside in order to gesture with her hands. "You can't take Cody on a car ride, then to a rodeo, by yourself."

"My brother will be with us."

"And how much experience does he have with children?"

"Mariana—"

"Do not pull rank on me again. Please," she implored. "We're not talking about a family dinner."

"I have to compete. I can't afford to miss another weekend."

She stiffened. "Of course not."

He started to say he wasn't like her father, then stopped. To her, he must look and sound exactly like Zeb Snow.

"I'll just stay home and watch Cody," she said.

Jacob didn't want to argue.

"Come with us. Just this once. Next week, we hire someone to watch Cody."

"A nanny?"

"Yeah. For weekends only. That way, you can get your work done."

She hesitated.

"I promise. You can have equal say in who we hire. More than equal say. What do I know about hiring a nanny?"

"I could talk to my boss about taking half a day off." She prodded a piece of orange chicken with her chopsticks. "I am due a ton of vacation time."

"And you've been putting in really long hours at the office."

"We'll see." She resumed eating.

She hadn't exactly conceded, but Jacob let himself enjoy the small victory anyway. He still had three days to seal the deal.

They were finishing dinner when Jacob's cell phone chimed, alerting him to an email. He automatically tensed as he had every day this week. Would the DNA testing facility be sending the results this late in the day?

Seconds later, Mariana's cell phone beeped from her purse on the counter.

"That's weird," she said, then, as if realization dawned, looked at him before leaping from her chair.

Jacob got to his phone first and checked the screen. His heart lurched upon reading the name of the sender.

"It's from the lab," Mariana said from behind him, her voice thready.

The email font was tiny. Jacob had to expand the message to locate the embedded link. It took him three attempts to type in the password he'd chosen.

And there it was. The results. In big bold letters with a disclaimer that the test results were 99 percent accurate.

"I guess we know for sure now." Mariana expelled a long breath. "Leah was telling the truth."

"Yes, we know." Jacob waited, giving himself a moment to fully process the ramifications. Mariana sat back down, but she didn't meet his gaze. Cody slammed his fists on the high chair tray, his way of saying he was done and wanted down.

"I'll get him."

Before she could move, Jacob reached for her hand. "Wait."

"What's wrong?"

"There's something I want to talk to you about."

She looked at him then, visibly on edge. "Besides the rodeo?"

"I want full custody of Cody. Not shared."

"Full," she repeated.

"I'm not going to be a part-time father. Cody deserves more, and I'm going to see he has it."

Chapter 6

"What, Mom? Oh, no!" Mariana sat in the rear seat of Jacob's truck with Cody beside her, her mother on the phone. They were well on their way to Austin, only about an hour from the city limits. "I understand. Don't worry, it's okay. Your feeling better is what's important. I don't know yet." She caught Jacob's glance in the rearview mirror. "Let me see."

"What's wrong?" Jacob asked when she'd disconnected.

"Mom came down with Grandma's cold. She woke up with a sore throat and a runny nose."

"That's a shame."

"She doesn't want Cody and me to come. She's afraid we'll get sick, too."

Selfishly, Mariana didn't want either her or Cody to succumb. Caring for a sick toddler was no picnic. He'd have to stay home from day care, and with so much to do at work, she couldn't take any more personal time off. Two days last week and today had put her behind. She'd been able to make a few phone calls while Cody napped, but not review the notes she'd made on her tablet or study the briefs she'd downloaded. She'd been hoping to tackle those while her mother babysat.

"We'll book you a hotel room where we're staying," Jacob offered.

"I don't suppose we could go back home."

Both men cranked their heads around to gape at her.

"Bad suggestion?" she asked weakly.

Jacob returned his gaze to the road.

Daniel cast him a sidelong look. "We might not make it in time to compete in tonight's events."

She tried to brush off his remark. Daniel wasn't a mean guy. He actually seemed pretty nice. The resemblance between the brothers was undeniable. In more ways than one. They both placed rodeoing high on their priority lists. Like her father. She was, she thought with aggravation, surrounded by them.

"What about taking a shuttle back?"

Mariana considered Jacob's suggestion for a nanosecond, deciding she'd rather stick pins in her eyes than ride public transportation with what was bound to be a cranky two-year-old. Her fellow passengers would hate her.

"I don't think so."

"A rental car?"

That sounded like an ordeal. The day had already been a long one, and it was barely ten-thirty.

She laid her head back, resigning herself to the inevitable. These two cowboys weren't turning back for anything, and her other options were unappealing.

"The hotel room it is, I guess." Luckily, they'd packed Cody's portable crib and stroller.

Only then did she remember she wouldn't have any means of getting around. Drat. Stuck in a hotel room for the entire weekend. How exactly again had she wound up in this predicament?

She'd agreed, that was how. The morning after Jacob suggested she and Cody ride along and his announcement that he wanted full custody. She was still reeling from that, though in hindsight, she should have seen it coming. Instead, she'd convinced herself he was more like her father. Wrong.

For Cody's sake, she was happy. As long as Jacob didn't fail him. She'd miss her nephew terribly, of course. Common sense told her he had no intention of phasing either her or her mother out of Cody's life. They'd always be his family, the keepers of Leah's memories. Cody would know her through the stories they told him.

Mariana wiped away a stray tear. It had been her plan to tell her mother in person about Jacob assuming full custody. News like that deserved to be delivered face-to-face, not in a phone call. Only now, she and Cody weren't going to Austin.

"About that rental car..."

As it turned out, they didn't make it to the hotel. Not right away. While Daniel called to book a second room and advise the front desk of their late check-in, Jacob drove them directly to the fairgrounds. She bit her lower lip rather than complain. It would do no good. The brothers were on a mission.

On the plus side, Cody was content munching on Froot Loops and not making a fuss. He began babbling up a storm when they pulled onto the rodeo grounds in Round Rock, the sight of so many trucks, trailers and horses exciting him.

"Migo, Migo." He grinned and pointed at a horse the same color as Amigo.

Mariana had to admit, she, too, was a little fascinated by all the goings-on. She'd been to rodeos, of course. As a teenager to watch Leah compete. Back then, it had been torture. A place her mother dragged her against her will. While Leah had competed, Mariana buried her nose in a book.

How was it her mother had hated Mariana's father always being away at some rodeo but she'd fully supported Leah? Maybe, thought Mariana, her mother didn't dislike rodeos as much as she'd disliked her husband. It was something to consider and perhaps inquire about when the time was right.

They parked in the participants' lot. Because Jacob and Daniel hadn't trailered any horses, there was only Cody and his stroller to unload. Mariana grabbed her briefcase along with the diaper bag and hung both from the stroller's handle. If Jacob and Daniel took long doing whatever it was they needed to, she'd find a comfortable place to sit and review those briefs.

They crossed the dirt lot and made their way to the arena and registration booth. The stroller bumped and lurched. Mariana grunted as she pushed. Cody laughed.

Jacob materialized beside her. "Let me help."

She was instantly aware of him, as always of late. Ever since their kiss. Assuming his intentions were to ease her cumbersome load by carrying her briefcase and possibly the diaper bag, she was surprised when he took over steering the stroller.

"Thank you."

The sight of a tall, handsome cowboy pushing a stroller garnered plenty of female stares, hers included. He didn't look silly or out of place or put upon. He looked like a dad who pushed his son regularly and didn't mind. Mariana was sure hers wasn't the only heart melting.

The rodeo was not officially starting for a few more hours, but the grounds were already bustling with activity. Food and merchant vendors setting up. Maintenance staff running lines, checking equipment, grading the arena and testing the sound system. Livestock handlers moving calves and bucking stock to the holding pens. The local equestrian team—Mariana remembered a similar team from Leah's youth—practicing their opening ceremony drill in a distant field.

A tingle of anticipation wound through her as she took it all in. Soon, the stands would be packed and the participants competing, one of them Jacob. She knew from his and Daniel's conversation during the drive that he was entered in three events: saddle and bareback bronc riding and, of course, bull riding.

She was struck with a sudden urge to watch him compete. She hadn't seen him in action before, having arrived at the Louisiana State Fair Rodeo for their initial meeting well after he was done.

Once Jacob and Daniel had registered and were given their numbers, Daniel said to Jacob, "Let's check out the bulls and horses we've drawn."

"I will. Later. First, I'm taking Mariana and Cody to the hotel."

Giving up his chance to check out the livestock? Mariana was impressed.

"It's all right. You go on. Cody and I will keep busy."

Jacob studied her. "Are you sure?"

"We'll get something to eat. Maybe find an out-of-the-way place where I can work for a while." She marveled at her willingness to stick around even as the words spilled from her mouth. Thirty minutes ago, she'd been silently complaining.

"Thanks." His gaze was tender and, dare she think it, fond.

She found her lips curving upward in return. "No problem."

He came around to the front of the stroller, leaned down and tugged on the brim of Cody's ball cap. "See you later, pal. Take care of your aunt Mariana for me."

"Bye-bye." Cody extended his hand and squeezed his fingers in his version of a wave.

Mariana resumed pushing the stroller. "Call me later."

Before she quite realized what was happening, Jacob gave her cheek a peck. "For luck."

Her whole face instantly warmed. After that, he and Daniel sauntered off as if their entire worlds hadn't just tilted on their axis. Mariana's certainly had.

She watched Jacob's form grow smaller until he disappeared behind a metal building, the warmth spread until it reached all the way to her fingertips and toes.

"Cody, your aunt Mariana might be in a bit of trouble."

"Bye-bye."

"Yeah, bye-bye good sense."

She located a picnic table in the large awning-covered food court. By some miracle, she managed to work while Cody played with the toys she'd brought. More work was accomplished while he dozed in his stroller. She probably let him sleep too long and would pay for it tonight when he'd be up late, but she finished everything she'd hoped to, which relieved her stress enormously.

Her last task was to link the tablet's Wi-Fi to her phone's hot spot and email the revised briefs to her boss. She'd put a lot of effort into them. If all went as planned, the briefs would assist her team in convincing Paulo Molinas to offer a *decent* settlement.

When Jacob called to check on her and Cody, she cut him off before he could suggest she return to the hotel.

"When's your first event?"

Next thing she knew, she and Cody were sitting in the stands, cheering with the crowd as the equestrian team entered the arena and the opening ceremony got under way.

Jacob did only mediocre, placing sixth in bareback bronc riding and eighth in saddle bronc riding. The day was still young, Mariana told herself. Bull riding was the last event of the evening, and she crossed her fingers he'd do better.

Despite the late hour, Cody was still awake. The noise level alone would have kept Rip van Winkle from his slumber. At times Cody sat quietly in her lap. More frequently, he fussed. She hoped her supply of toddler treats held out. Breaking one of her strictest rules, she gave him sips of her sugar-infused lemonade. The straw fascinated him.

"Is his father competing?" The grandmotherly woman sitting beside Mariana beamed at Cody.

"Yes. Number twenty-seven."

The woman referred to her program. "Jacob Baron. Ah."

Mariana didn't quite know what to make of the "ah" so let it pass.

"I follow all the top-ranked cowboys," the woman said by way of explanation. "He's doing well this year. You must be proud."

What to say that wouldn't cause the woman to jump to the wrong conclusion? "Qualifying for Nationals is important to him."

"Don't you worry, he'll make it at the rate he's going."

Was Jacob thinking the same thing or worried about his so-so performance in bronc riding?

"I didn't realize he was married and had a son." Mariana was sure the woman stared at her left hand, searching for a ring.

"We're not married."

Another "ah" followed.

Mariana drew Cody closer. "I'm his aunt."

"The boy's mother couldn't make it?" The woman clucked sympathetically.

Okay, she was being just a little too nosy. Time to put an end to it. Mariana stood, balancing Cody on her hip and smiled so as not to offend the woman. "Excuse us just a minute. We have some pressing personal business to attend to." To emphasize her point, she patted Cody's bottom and grabbed the diaper bag.

Mariana squeezed past the people in the bleachers. By the time she reached the last row, she was wishing she hadn't returned the stroller to the truck.

She made it back just in time to see Jacob compete in bull riding. Her seat wasn't too far from the bucking chutes. She swore that he searched the stands for her as he straddled the side of the chute, right before climbing onto the bull's back. When his gaze appeared to land on her and Cody, she gave a wave and then pointed.

"Look! There's Daddy."

"Daddy, Daddy," Cody called out, twisting side to side and looking about as if he expected Jacob to come walking up.

Her stomach in knots, she watched and waited for the chute door to open. All at once, it did. The bull, a huge, nasty brute, lunged into the arena, dirt flying as he kicked out his back legs. He achieved unbelievable height. How could Jacob possibly hold on?

And then, he didn't. The entire stands gasped in unison as Jacob flew off the bull's back and hit the ground like a sack of stones.

Mariana was instantly up, a hand clasped to her mouth. My God, was he all right? What should she do? Stay? Run to him? Just as she started to move, Jacob pushed to his knees. Then, he, too, was standing. Reaching for his fallen hat, he brushed off his jeans as he strode toward the gate. He didn't even look back to make sure the bull was rounded up and the coast clear.

"Hey, folks, let's give this here cowboy a hand," the announcer's voice blared from the speakers. "That's all he's going to take home tonight."

"There's always tomorrow," the woman beside Mariana said brightly.

At the end of the day during the ride to the hotel, Jacob said little. Mariana left him alone, recognizing his need to brood. He did see her and Cody to her room, but there was no goodnight peck on the cheeks. One thing went well, however. The instant she settled Cody in the portable crib, he fell soundly asleep.

Sticking around the hotel room on Saturday and Sunday didn't appeal to her, so Mariana and Cody went with Jacob and Daniel to the rodeo. She planned on getting more work done but actually accomplished nothing. In truth, she had fun. It had been a long time since she took a weekend simply for herself, and in the end, she was really glad she came.

Jacob was another story. He didn't appear to be having any fun at all and qualified for only one event during the final rounds on Sunday. He squeaked by with fourth place in bareback bronc riding, which wasn't going to help him much in his rankings.

The worse he performed, the more withdrawn he became until he was hardly talking at all—though he continued to search out Mariana and Cody before each event.

As they were leaving, she overheard Daniel talking to another cowboy, saying, "I'm not sure what's messing with his head this weekend. I just hope he gets over it soon."

Something had definitely thrown Jacob off his game. The answer was revealed during the tense drive home when he abruptly announced, "We need to hire that nanny right away. Before this coming weekend. That way, you and Cody can stay home."

Huh. Apparently he wasn't nearly as glad as she was that she and Cody had tagged along all weekend. Mariana tried to ignore the hurt and disappointment she felt, but it sat like a heavy weight in the pit of her stomach.

"She's not the one."

"Why? I liked her."

Mariana shook her head. "She wasn't friendly enough. When Cody showed her his trick with Buster, she just patted his head and said he was a clever boy."

Jacob almost laughed out loud but managed to contain himself. "You intimidated her. I think she felt like she was being cross-examined on the witness stand rather than interviewing for a nanny position."

"My point. If she can't stand up to a little pressure, how's she going to handle a rambunctious toddler?"

Mariana tossed her overnight bag onto her bed, then went to the closet and flipped through the clothes hanging there as if they were items on a clearance rack. Cody knelt on the floor, playing with her shoes, sticking one inside the other and squealing with frustration when they didn't fit. He'd been cranky since waking up.

Jacob observed them both from where he stood in the doorway to her bedroom, maintaining his distance out of respect for her privacy. Also because being in such close proximity to her caused him to feel certain things. Things that had nothing to do with their present conversation and everything to do with…well, proximity.

"She came highly recommended from the agency."

"She's not right," Mariana repeated.

"You didn't like the other three, either."

"That first one was too shy. We need a nanny with confidence."

"Didn't you see her knees knocking together? You terrified her."

"I'm not that bad." Mariana selected a power suit—what else?—and after folding it neatly, packed it in the bag. At least this suit had a skirt and not pants. The lucky client she was meeting, an elderly military veteran Jacob had been told, would get to see her legs.

"I was hoping to have someone hired by today," he said.

There were only a few weekends left before Nationals. With his dismal showing at the Lucky Draw, his rankings had dropped marginally. Any lower was unacceptable. Knowing Cody was being safely supervised by a qualified professional—at home—would go a long way in easing his mind.

It would ease Mariana's mind, too. She was nervous about leaving Cody with Jacob for this one simple overnight trip to consult with the elderly client in Houston.

"I'll call the agency and set up more interviews for tomorrow evening," she said. "I should be home by six at the latest."

They'd seen three women yesterday evening and one this morning. Jacob was thinking the whole interviewing process had gone on long enough. Any of the candidates the agency had sent would do a fine job. This one today, Simone, was more than fine. She was a sweet, quiet woman in her forties. Mother of two mostly grown children whom, from all accounts, she'd neither maimed nor killed while raising.

Jacob made a snap decision. "In the meantime, Leeza can help. She lives right next door, and she's available."

"She's thirteen."

"And qualified."

"Watching a dog doesn't require the same skill level as watching a child."

"She babysits her younger cousins. And Cody likes her." The girl had been over twice since Cody and Mariana came to live with Jacob, lavishing attention on the boy to the extent where Buster sulked from jealousy.

"Because she plays with him." Mariana zipped her bag closed.

"Isn't that what babysitters do?"

"Playing is only a small part of the job."

"She knows CPR. She went through babysitting training. Has a certificate and everything. She showed me."

"Doggie CPR?"

"Not funny." Actually, it was funny. He'd give her that.

"Well, CPR training is something," Mariana conceded. "She can't, however, drive a car if Cody needs to be taken to the emergency room."

"Her parents can. Besides, we're just talking this Saturday and Sunday while I'm gone and you're here," Jacob said as if the arrangement was a done deal, which in his mind, it was. "We don't want a repeat of last weekend."

"Fine." Mariana lifted the overnight bag and slung the strap over her shoulder. "But only because my mom's still not feeling well. Or I'd ask her to come up and watch Cody." At the mention of her mother, Mariana's voice grew tight.

Swell. She was still smarting from his needless and careless remarks this past weekend. Jacob had screwed up for sure. It wasn't her fault he'd performed like someone at their first professional rodeo. Nor was it her fault that every glimpse of her and Cody in the stands shattered his concentration. Yet he'd treated her as if it was.

Jacob could connect the dots; he wasn't that stupid. Their inability to agree on a nanny had something, if not everything, to do with her hurt feelings. Not that she was being vengeful or spiteful. Obstinate maybe.

An apology would probably go a long way in improving her attitude, except he couldn't quite form the words.

"You will call me if you need anything." She stood facing him, indecision written all over her face. She didn't want to leave Cody alone with Jacob.

"We'll be fine."

He'd made arrangements to go into work late so that he could be there for the interview and drop off Cody at day care, which was a good half hour out of his way. He'd also be leaving work early in order to pick Cody up. The need to find a nanny was becoming even more pressing. One who could drive.

"I put the list of emergency phone numbers on the refrigerator." Mariana reached for Cody's hand. He protested loudly, objecting at having to leave the shoes.

"I saw." Jacob stood aside so Mariana, Cody and her bulky bag could pass.

She recited items as she walked. "There's an unopened box of diapers in the closet. A clean set of crib sheets in the top dresser drawer in case his diaper leaks during the night. And, please, please, limit the junk food."

"Here I thought the two of us would slam

back a few beers with our pizza while we watched the game."

"I'm serious, Jacob." They had reached the front door.

"I know."

She'd go on forever if he let her, and she had a meeting to make. Jacob reached for her bag. "I'll carry this to the car. You get Cody."

She watched as he stowed her bag in the rear seat of the Infiniti. Cody stood at the edge of the driveway, already waving and saying, "Bye-bye, Mama."

Her face crumpled. Was she going to cry?

"Hey, are you okay?" Jacob wondered if he should put an arm around her shoulder or something.

"It's nothing."

"I'm sorry about being such a jerk this weekend. I don't like losing and shouldn't have taken it out on you."

"Wow. That's quite an ego you have." She sniffed and squared her shoulders. "Did you really just make this all about you?"

Three strikes. He was definitely out.

"I'll call you after I've dropped Cody off at day care."

"And when you pick him up," she added, kissing Cody goodbye. Jacob got a brief hug.

They waited until she was down the road before going inside. The stars must have been perfectly aligned, for Cody behaved like a champ, and they were out the door in record time. At day care, he gave Jacob the same wave he had Mariana.

"Bye-bye, Daddy."

The young woman attendant smiled broadly. "He looks just like you."

Did he? Jacob studied Cody's face, unable to see himself in it. "Thanks."

"Hug," Cody insisted.

"Sure thing." Jacob bent and pulled Cody close. The boy's small arms circled his neck. It was a nice feeling. "You be good. See you later."

"See you."

The workday progressed without incident, thanks to more aligned stars. Jacob attended a meeting with visiting executives, one of them Jet, and tried not to let his brother's position in upper management annoy him. Instead, he turned his emotions inward, using them to fuel his motivation to do well at the Rough and Ready Rodeo this coming weekend in McAlester.

Pushing paper occupied a good hour of his time. After that, he walked the rig and conferred with the various foremen. His last tasks of the day were reviewing requisition forms and answering emails.

He considered calling the day care again and decided once at lunch was sufficient. Funny, he hadn't done that before, call the day care. Then again, this was his first time in charge of "transportation" as Mariana had referred to it. When he'd spoken to the day care at lunch, the gal answering the phone informed him that Mariana had also called. He should have expected that.

Leaving work a little later than he'd hoped to, he made it to the day care just minutes before six o'clock when the dreaded penalty charges kicked in. Mariana had warned him extensively to be on time. He figured she was more concerned about poor Cody being stuck waiting and not the money.

While the two of them did catch part of the game on TV, there was no beer and pizza. Cody fussed over his packaged toddler meal, which was unusual for him. Jacob took a taste and didn't blame the kid. The stuff would choke a snake. He offered cereal, but Cody also refused that. Eventually, he gave Cody a bath and put him to bed.

An hour later, just as Jacob was getting

ready for bed himself, Cody woke up crying and he didn't stop. After forty minutes, Jacob called Mariana, telling her about the crying and Cody's lack of appetite at dinner.

"He could be teething again," she said. "I should have figured that out this morning when he was so cranky. Open his mouth and take a look."

Jacob pinched Cody's chin between his thumb and forefinger and pried open his mouth. The boy didn't make it easy. "Hard to really tell."

"There's some teething gel in the diaper bag. Try that and see if it helps. If not, call me back. Call me back anyway," she added, a note of concern in her voice.

The gel did help, and Jacob reported the good news when he called.

"I'm glad." She sounded tired.

"Get some sleep. You've got an early morning."

After all the fuss, Cody simply wasn't in the mood for bed. Jacob sat on the couch with his feet up, watching Cody play with Buster on the floor and trying not to doze off.

He obviously failed for when his phone chimed sometime later, he jerked awake. Luckily, Cody was perfectly fine. No playing with matches or sticking his fingers in electrical sockets. Ingenious tyke that he was, he'd made an obstacle course out of blocks and Buster's front legs and was driving his truck through it, complete with sound effects.

God, Jacob thought, what if something had happened while he slept? He tried not to dwell on that as he checked his phone's display and answered the call. It was Darius, the night shift safety supervisor, on the line.

"What's going on?" Jacob asked. Darius didn't call without a good reason.

"Lenny Bartholomy fell from the catwalk."

"Is he hurt?"

"Banged his head pretty hard and appears to have sprained his ankle."

Jacob sat up straight. "Did he lose consciousness?"

"No, but he's light-headed and complaining of pain. I'm getting ready to take him to the emergency room."

"Report back to me when you get there. I'm heading to the drill site now. If I need to, I'll meet you at the hospital." As senior safety manager, Jacob was required to inspect the accident scene, talk to witnesses, if any, write a report and make sure protocol was followed. If the injury had been minor, he'd wait until the morning. But this one was necessitating a trip to the hospital. "Have a drug test administered as soon as possible."

Jacob didn't think Lenny was using, but testing was mandatory in every accident case. No exceptions.

"Will do," Darius said. "But in my opinion, he just wasn't paying attention and slipped. Seems his girlfriend just told him she was pregnant."

Sudden fatherhood, Jacob knew firsthand, could mess with a guy's concentration.

He stood, looking about for the work boots he kicked off earlier…and his gaze landed on Cody. What was he going to do with him? Too late to ask Leeza to babysit, and the day care wasn't open.

What did Luke do with Rosie? Jacob didn't have to call his friend for the answer. He'd seen Luke bring Rosie to the Roughneck more than once in the middle of the night.

"Come on, son. Looks like we're going for a ride." Lifting Cody into his arms, Jacob started for Mariana's room where the boy's jacket hung on the back of chair. "You're gonna get to see where your old man works."

Chapter 7

Jacob's work truck stood in the driveway. Good, he was home. Mariana would have called ahead except she'd already called him four times today and had run out of excuses. During each conversation he had assured her Cody was fine and that the teething episode appeared to have run its course.

She paused at the front door before entering. When was the last time she'd thought of her own house, the east half of a cozy duplex? Yesterday. When the neighbors she'd asked to keep an eye on the place let her know everything was fine. Then, poof. All thoughts of her residence vanished as she'd concentrated on work.

Perhaps this new routine of hers had become too familiar. Too comfortable. She and Cody could probably do with a little shaking up. Better yet, a change of scenery.

Jacob was busy competing this weekend. No reason not to take Cody to her house. They could spend the night. She didn't want him to forget about her home after she moved out.

Or was it Cody forgetting about *her* she most feared? Mariana pushed the dreadful and can't-possibly-be-true thought from her mind.

"Hello!" She shut the door behind her.

"In here," Jacob answered from the kitchen.

Good grief, he was fixing dinner again. Guilt stopped her in her tracks. She was taking entirely too much advantage of him. Their arrangement should be fifty-fifty. She didn't like feeling indebted to him.

A tempting aroma assaulted her upon entering the kitchen, matched only by the equally tempting sight of Jacob. There was something very appealing about a big masculine man puttering around the kitchen.

"You made it. How was the trip?" He smiled, and instantly went from appealing to heart-stoppingly sexy.

Suddenly, her overnight bag was too heavy to hold. Mariana set it on the floor at her feet, needing a moment to collect her wits before answering.

"Great. Signed another client."

"Your boss must be happy."

"He is." Which made Mariana happy. Had she done enough to move her name up on that short list for junior partner? Possibly.

Buster had come over to greet her, but there was no sign of her nephew.

"Where's Cody?"

Jacob stepped aside. Cody stood on a chair at the sink, the sprayer in his hand.

"Hi, hi!" Grinning with glee, he blasted the cups and dishes in the basin with water.

Mariana rushed forward. "My God, Jacob. What are you thinking? He'll fall."

"I'll have you know, I'm senior safety manager at Baron Energies' largest and most productive drill site. Do you think for one second I'd take a chance with my son?"

He turned, and Mariana saw it then. Cody was tethered to Jacob with some sort of belt device. He also wore a plastic hard hat that was too big for his head and a fluorescent-yellow nylon vest with reflective tape down the sides. Jacob had evidently brought all manner of goodies home from work.

"It's a harness," he explained, jerking on the strap to demonstrate its strength. "No way can Cody fall."

"Mama!" Without missing a beat, Cody pointed the sprayer at Mariana and let loose with a stream of water.

She ducked, but not in time. Her suit jacket took the worst of the damage.

"Hey!" Jacob used his hand to aim the nozzle down. "What did I say earlier? No spraying people or animals."

Rather than cry or whimper at the stern reprimand, Cody laughed. "Gotcha!"

"Yeah, gotcha," Jacob repeated.

Mariana stared. A new word. This game must have been going on for a while before she arrived.

"Hi to you, too." She went over to Cody and, brushing his hair aside, kissed him on the forehead.

"Hug," he insisted.

She gave him one, then straightened—and bumped into Jacob, who was only inches from Cody thanks to the harness.

"Sorry," she muttered.

"Welcome home." His voice had taken on a

husky quality she hadn't heard before. There was also a glint in his eyes.

"No hug for me?"

She gave him a clumsy, one-armed excuse for a hug. "I should change." Ducking around him, she grabbed her overnight bag from the floor. "Then I'll help."

"No rush."

In her room, away from Jacob's potent appeal, she could once again think clearly.

No rush?

Of course not. Jacob had handled the teething incident as well as survived a full twenty-four hours taking care of Cody mostly without her assistance. Not that she approved of the whole standing on a chair, even with a harness. But it showed he was considering Cody's welfare.

Mariana caught a glimpse of herself in the mirror as she tugged on a sweatshirt over the jeans she'd donned. When had she gone from busy, single, self-absorbed attorney who saw her nephew only when she visited to a worry-wart guardian? More startling than that was how fast the change had occurred.

"Hope you don't mind slightly overdone rolls?" Jacob asked. He'd tucked Cody under his arm as if he were holding a football. With his free hand, he removed a pan from the oven.

She rushed forward. "I'll get that."

Transferring the pan and hot pads turned out to be more awkward than she'd anticipated. Hands and arms brushed during the exchange. Gazes locked.

"Down, down." Cody's demand was punctuated with giggles.

Mariana hurried the steaming pan to the counter, setting it on the wooden cutting board. Jacob untethered Cody and lowered him to the floor. He immediately went for a tape measure under the table and began extracting the tape.

"What other stuff did you bring from work today?" she asked as Jacob spooned a ground turkey casserole from the Crock-Pot.

"I actually brought the stuff home last night. I figured it'd keep Cody busy on the drive, only he fell asleep."

"That might be part of the reason he was so cranky last evening. If he sleeps on the way home from day care, he doesn't want to go to bed at his regular time." She lifted Cody, who still clutched the tape measure, and stuffed him into the high chair.

When she went to remove the hard hat, he grabbed the brim with both hands. "No!"

She opted to leave well enough alone. Did it really matter if he wore the hard hat during dinner?

"Oh, he didn't sleep on the way home from day care." Jacob carried the casserole to the table. "This was on the way back from the drill site."

She spun around. "I don't understand."

"I got a call about ten. One of my men fell from the catwalk."

"You took Cody to the drill site?"

"Yeah."

"At ten o'clock at night?"

"What else was I supposed to do?"

She spoke slowly, one word at a time. "Get someone else."

"I'm the senior safety manager."

"He's two."

"It was an emergency."

Her voice rose. "A child has no business being at a drill site."

"He wasn't at the actual drill. I was careful. I didn't put him down once. And—" Jacob gestured toward Cody "—as you can see, he's fine."

Wasn't that just like a guy? No one was

hurt, which automatically made everything okeydokey.

"Th-this can not h-happen again." She was stuttering. Dammit! He'd made her that mad.

"I agree." Jacob sat down and pointed to the chair she normally occupied. When she didn't move—how could she, really?—he said, "Which is why I called the agency today and hired Simone."

The unfriendly gal they'd interviewed yesterday morning.

Mariana didn't sit in the chair, she slid onto it.

"She lives close and is willing to come over when there's an emergency. I verified before offering her the job."

And like that, it was settled. Jacob had decided. He'd been faced with a dilemma and solved it. Without her input or consideration.

Evidently, she hadn't given him enough credit. Or gave herself too much.

"Okay, sweetie. Quit your wiggling."

Cody didn't oblige and thwarted Mariana's every attempt at putting him into his coat.

"Here, give me that." She reached for the five-by-seven photo clutched in his hand.

"No." He smashed the photo to his chest. "Santa."

He'd been carrying the photo for hours, like a treasured possession. Even napping with it. The edges were bent and a crease cut diagonally across the middle.

Though it was much, much too early in Mariana's opinion, her mother had driven up from Austin bright and early that morning, insisting they take Cody to the mall for a picture with Santa Claus. She wanted it for her Christmas cards. Mariana had been appalled at the price Santa's helper had charged them. However, after seeing the adorable picture, they'd stopped off at the local drugstore with its photo station and had copies made.

Mariana had given Jacob two, one for himself and another for his family. He'd scowled but accepted the photos. The Barons, it seemed, were a touchy subject these days. Brock Baron, to be specific. The family patriarch wasn't happy with Jacob's inability to qualify for Nationals and was letting him know it.

That morning, Mariana had unintentionally caught part of what was clearly a terse phone conversation between the two men. Jacob had avoided her after that, which annoyed Mariana more than a little. They were supposed to be finding a new day care facility in the area. Once she moved out, taking Cody to and from day care was going to fall entirely on Jacob. The pamphlets Mariana had collected sat in plain sight on the counter and after three days remained undisturbed.

Despite that, she was determined to have equal vote in the final choice. Not that the nanny he'd hired wasn't nice, and she did come highly recommended. And Jacob had been right to have reliable backup should he be called to the drill site on another emergency again. But she wanted a say in the decisions affecting Cody.

Get over it. You won't be here much longer.

Wherever that small, annoying voice came from, it needed to shut up. She was here now, and until the day she left, she'd see to it that Jacob did right by Cody in every way.

Which was why she was going with Jacob and Cody tonight to the Harvest Festival with Carly, Luke and his daughter Rosie. Jacob hadn't delivered any kind of ultimatum. His "Please come with us" invitation sounded sincere, but Mariana couldn't help feeling that he would take Cody regardless of how she felt, and she could either go or stay.

As a result, she was now attempting to ready Cody for the evening. He insisted on wearing his favorite denim jacket. Mariana might not have minded, except it had turned cold the past few days. She wanted Cody in something warmer, but he'd have none of it.

His squeals of protest must have traveled across the hall because Jacob, also home early, appeared in the doorway of Mariana's room. "Everything okay?"

"Peachy." She rubbed a throbbing temple and sat back on her calves, having resorted to kneeling in front of Cody to better control his squirming and wiggling. "Cody refuses to wear anything but his denim jacket, and it's too cold for that."

"Hey, partner." Jacob stepped into the room, both arms held behind his back. "I'll make you a deal."

Cody stared up at him with wide eyes.

"You do what your aunt Mariana wants, and I'll let you wear these." He pulled out a pair of child-size cowboy boots from behind his back.

"Boots!" Cody lunged for them, pushing past Mariana.

Jacob held them out of reach. "Nope. Only if you put on your warm jacket. Then, and only then, you can have this, too." He brought out his other arm, which held a stick pony.

The deal was struck. Cody donned the warm coat in record time, and Jacob relinquished the bounty.

"What every buckaroo needs," he said as Cody stood before them, wearing his new boots and sitting astride his new toy.

Mariana thought Jacob had gone a little overboard with the boots. Cody didn't really know the difference between them and his sneakers. The stick pony, with its plush head and yarn mane, was pretty cute. Cody loved it and immediately named it Migo. What else?

They met Luke, Carly and Rosie in the parking lot of the community church where the Harvest Festival was being held. It started daily at three o'clock and closed at eight. They were late. It was now five. But they made it in time for the last hayride, which the children loved, and the petting zoo. Rosie was terrified of the goats, who nibbled on the buttons of her coat. Cody took Migo with him and rode the stick pony everywhere. Endless pictures were snapped.

After an exhausting two hours, which included three trips to the pumpkin patch and one to the craft tables, they finished with a round of hot chocolate at the concession stand. The two toddlers huddled together at the picnic table. They were sandwiched between Jacob on one side and Carly on the other, sharing a hot chocolate and, this was a nice change, not fighting.

Mariana sat across from Jacob, holding her foam cup between her hands and using it to warm them. In their rush to leave, she'd forgotten gloves.

"Are you competing this weekend?" Luke asked Jacob.

"Yeah. Daniel's going, too."

"What about Jet?"

"He's done for the year. Jasmine and her girls are keeping him pretty busy."

Mariana watched Jacob's face, glad to see his expression relaxed. He could talk about rodeoing again without clenching his teeth. From what he'd told her, he had exactly two more rodeos before Nationals. If he performed well, he could still qualify.

Talk eventually moved to the upcoming holidays.

"Do you have any plans for Thanksgiving?" Carly wanted to know.

"I haven't thought that far ahead," Mariana admitted.

What would happen? She'd like to take

Cody to her mother's. Jacob probably had his own ideas.

Mariana absently stirred her hot chocolate with a small plastic stir straw, and tried not to dwell on how devastated her mother would be not to spend the holiday with her only grandchild. Maybe she and Jacob could compromise.

"We always host a huge dinner. Really nice." Carly sent Jacob an arch look. "This year, there's going to be even more people."

Was she hinting at him inviting Mariana? What would she say if he asked?

"I haven't thought that far ahead, either." Jacob caught Mariana's eye.

Who were they kidding? Thanksgiving was just around the corner.

"We'll see," she answered lightly. No way was she discussing Thanksgiving and who got custody of Cody at the festival and certainly not in front of Jacob's sister and future brother-in-law.

"Aiiee!" The squeal came from Cody, who'd somehow managed to tip over his cup of hot chocolate. The dark puddle headed for the edge of the picnic table—and his lap—at an alarming rate. Rosie started to cry.

Mariana jumped up, ready to run to the

rescue. She didn't get two steps before Jacob whipped out a stack of paper napkins and sopped up the mess, including the small amount that had dribbled onto Cody.

"Here you go." Jacob took Cody's cup and filled it with some hot chocolate from his own.

"Tank you," Cody said, all smiles. Next, he tilted his head sideways and laid it against Jacob's arm.

"Aw." Carly smiled tenderly. "How cute."

Mariana's heart tore clean in half. She was also affected by the charming display between father and son. But she was wounded, too. Her role as her nephew's primary caregiver and parent was coming to an end, and Mariana dreaded the day. He was the last link to her sister.

Jacob needs me, she told herself. He wasn't ready to parent Cody alone, but at the rate he was going, he would be soon.

Chapter 8

In the parking lot, they made their farewells. While the men shook hands, Carly pulled Mariana into a hug.

"Come to Thanksgiving dinner at the Roughneck," she said.

"Thanks again for the invite," Mariana hedged, wishing she didn't have to.

Both children were whiny, a combination of too much excitement and fast approaching bedtime.

"Wanna go," Cody complained.

As expected, he fell asleep on the way home. She and Jacob didn't talk much and when they did, they kept their voices low.

"Did you have a good time?" he asked. The truck idled as they waited at a stoplight.

"Very good. Carly and Luke are nice."

"I hope she didn't put you on the spot about Thanksgiving dinner."

"She didn't."

"Uh-huh." Jacob chuckled.

"I don't mind."

"Have you thought about it?"

"Not really." Such a lie.

"Would your mother be willing to drive up? If not, we could drive down to see her."

Mariana turned in her seat to look at him. "You'd do that?"

"Sure."

"What about your family?"

"I can see them anytime."

Was he letting his disagreement with Brock affect his plans? Did she care?

"That would be nice." Because he'd offered a concession, she made one, too. "Maybe she could come here and bring Grandma. I'd hate for you to miss the Baron get-together."

"They can come to the Roughneck with us."

"Maybe. That might be too much for Grandma. She's hard of hearing and has trouble in large groups with lots of commotion."

"Then we'll have two dinners. Or just one. At home with them."

Mariana promptly chided herself. She'd been much too hard on Jacob earlier and too quick to judge him. He was being very considerate, not excluding her and her family at all. That would teach her.

Jacob carried a sleeping Cody into the house. He didn't wake, even when they put him in his pajamas. Mariana laid him in the crib while Jacob watched. There was very little room to maneuver; the crib occupied all the available space. She and Jacob were forced to stand close. He smelled like fresh air, having brought the outdoors inside with him.

What about her? Did he like how she smelled? Did he ever look at her like a woman and not his housemate? They'd kissed once. Briefly. He'd kept his distance after that. She'd agreed it was for the best. That hadn't stopped her from remembering. And daydreaming.

She reached into the crib and pulled the blanket up to Cody's neck, then tucked it in, forming a snug cocoon in which he slept. "'Night, handsome."

Jacob moved aside. She waited at the door

to her room, unsure of what to do next. It wasn't exactly late, and there was plenty of work waiting for her. Documents to review. Correspondence to write. Emails to answer. Only she wasn't in the mood. She was still worried about her precarious place in Cody's life, pleased by Jacob's willingness to include her family at Thanksgiving and still a little mesmerized by how nice he smelled. Especially the latter.

"See you in the morning?" He paused, his broad shoulders all but filling the doorway and edging her out.

"Not unless you're going in late." She smiled. "Five is just too early for me."

"I had a nice time tonight." His tone was that of a man saying good-night to the woman he'd just brought home from a date.

Nothing could be further from the truth. Yet Mariana felt a familiar tingle. The one that preceded a kiss.

"Me, too," she whispered.

He nodded, and she waited for him to walk across the hall to his room. Except he didn't.

"Mariana..." He said her name soft and low.

The tingle was followed by another. Sensing what was coming, what he wanted, she tilted her face up to meet his mouth, already descending to claim hers.

The kiss was hot. Burning. Nothing at all like their previous, nearly chaste one. It threatened to consume her. After a token resistance, she let it.

He swept her into his arms. Hers circled his neck, drawing him even closer. She couldn't get enough of him. His taste. His touch. His very evident need for her. They all fed the fire intensifying between them. A groan emanated from deep inside his chest. It echoed the sound of contentment escaping her.

This was madness. Tomorrow, five minutes from now, she would regret their impulsiveness and lack of judgment. Now, however, she embraced the moment and Jacob. Arching into him, she urged him to deepen the kiss. He responded by taking bolder liberties with his tongue and letting his hands wander the length of her back.

After a moment, he settled them on her hips and fitted her more snugly to him. She almost gasped aloud. She was in heaven and didn't want to return to earth. Not yet.

When the need to draw a decent breath overwhelmed them, they broke apart. Common sense returned and, darn it all, prevailed.

"We should probably stop now while we still can." Did that ragged voice belong to her?

"Yeah." Jacob stepped back, but he didn't release her. Instead, he moved his hands to her waist, a place slightly safer than her hips.

They felt nice. Firm and strong and not too possessive. She'd have liked them to remain where they were for a while. It wasn't to be.

"We can't keep doing this," she said. "The situation is complicated."

"Not that complicated."

"I'm here, with you, only because you need my help with Cody."

He drew back as if offended, his hands falling from her waist. "That's not why I kissed you."

"I'm glad." She had to smile at that. It faded quickly. "I'm not sure of my place in Cody's life anymore."

"You're his aunt. The only mother he'll ever know."

"Yes, and you're his father. Would we be kissing if his custody hadn't brought us together?"

"Trust me, I'd find you attractive and want to kiss you regardless of how we met."

"Want to. But not necessarily do it. Face it, we aren't exactly each other's type."

"And clearly I've been wrong all these years to limit myself."

He touched the side of her face. The gesture was achingly sweet. She almost forgot the point she was trying to make.

"I think it's best for all of us, you, me and Cody, if we didn't get involved. Not now. Maybe later."

"Maybe?"

"You're rodeoing and will be at least until the end of the year. Not only do I think you should give that up for Cody, I…hesitate getting involved with a cowboy. Not after the hell my father put my mother through. I need someone more steady and more reliable. Cody, too."

"I'm those things. I promise."

"You can be."

"I will be. Give me a chance."

"We'll see."

When she averted her gaze, he captured her chin with his fingers and turned her face back to his. "Okay. We wait. I understand your reservations and respect them. But rest assured, once I win a title at Nationals, I'll be coming around again, Mariana Snow, to pick up where we left off."

He returned to his room then. Mariana

leaned against the closed door and counted to ten, willing her heart rate to return to normal. She didn't quit until she reached a hundred.

Next to riding a horse, hard work provided the best outlet for stress. Jacob had spent all day with his nose to the grindstone, first at the drill site and now here at home. Amigo was reaping the benefits. Another thirty minutes of shoveling manure into a wheelbarrow, and the horse's stall and paddock would be spotless.

Jacob doubled his efforts. Still, the knot of tension residing in the back of his neck didn't loosen. It had been there since last night when he'd kissed Mariana. Again.

Okay, any red-blooded man wouldn't blame him. She'd tempt a saint. Standing in the half-light of the bedroom, putting Cody to bed, their bodies had been close enough to share heat. Then, there was the look in her eyes when they said good-night. He'd been tempted, all right. To do a lot more than just kiss her over and over.

Had she not put the brakes on, he'd have suggested they go out on a date. Or walk across the hall to his room. In hindsight, she was right in stopping him. Her voice had changed when she'd started talking about them kissing only because of their current living situation and not being each other's type.

She had doubts, about him and his attraction to her. Also about his ability to be the kind of man she wanted and needed. He believed he was. All that was left was to prove it. He would. After Nationals in December and after he was promoted from the drill site to Baron Energies' corporate offices.

"Cody, come back here."

"Wanna dig."

"Not there." The lights in the paddock weren't nearly as good as those at the Roughneck. Cody could easily disappear into one of the many dark corners. "Stay by me."

Cody came, dragging a spade Jacob had found in the storage room.

The boy was playing more than helping. Mostly, he was stirring up dust. Buster lay nearby, mindless of the cloud wafting over him as Cody banged the spade into the ground.

Jacob shook his head and dumped another shovel load into the wheelbarrow. Mariana would probably go crazy if she knew Cody was playing in dirt. Dirt and manure. Jacob was doing his best to keep the boy clean. Only problem, his best wasn't very good.

Luckily, Mariana wasn't home to see how dirty Cody had gotten. She was working late at the office, something to do with the firm's case against Paulo Molinas and Medallion Investments. Jacob planned to have Cody bathed and in his pajamas long before she got home.

He'd let her put Cody to bed alone tonight, however. No way was he risking a repeat of last night. It was just as well he and Daniel were leaving tomorrow morning for the Verde Valley Pro Rodeo. He had to get his head in the game between now and then if he expected to bring home a win in at least two events.

"Hello!" Mariana's voice carried across the yard from the back door.

She was home early.

"Swell," Jacob muttered and dropped his shovel. "Cody, quick. Come here." He snatched up the boy, removed the spade from his grasp and brushed off his jacket, for all the good it did.

"Jacob, where are you?"

"Let me do all the talking, got it?" He set Cody on his feet. "We're here. In the paddock."

"Mama!" Cody ran toward the railing.

"Wow. You're filthy." Mariana stopped at

the railing to gape at him. "What in the world did you get into?"

"Digging!" Cody proclaimed gleefully. "Help Daddy."

"I see." She cast Jacob a stern look.

Jacob sauntered over, his gait nonchalant. "It's nothing that won't wash off."

"Thank goodness for that."

Cody returned to where Jacob had dropped the spade and resumed digging.

"Shouldn't you stop him?" she asked.

"At this point, I think it's a waste of time and energy." He grinned, hoping to win her over. "Lighten up, Mariana. Boys get dirty. It's a rite of passage."

She grimaced and held her nose. "There's more than dirt on him."

"That washes off, too. I should know, I've fallen in plenty during my life."

"I guess you're right." She visibly relaxed.

He was glad. "Tough day at the office?"

"Molinas's attorneys are putting up a fight. They've requested a third extension, citing that they need more time to locate a witness. It's all smoke and mirrors. In the meantime, our clients are suffering. Doing without the money he stole from them. As much as I believe in the justice system, sometimes the way it operates frustrates me."

There it was again, that passion she had for her work. She cared less about her potential promotion than the people she represented.

"You'll win," he said. "You have to."

"Getting there's the hard part." Finally, she smiled.

It was enough to make him forgot how cold it was outside. And here she was wearing only a thin nylon coat.

"It's chilly. You should go inside."

She hugged herself. "I'll take Cody. Give him that bath."

"You take a break. I'll do it. I'm the one who got him dirty. We're almost done here, anyway."

"We?" She raised her brows.

"You heard him, he's helping."

"If you say so." She peered around Jacob, suddenly frowning. "Where is he?"

"Right there." Jacob turned—and also frowned.

Cody was nowhere to be seen. Buster still lay by the wheelbarrow, his head resting on his paws.

"Cody," Jacob called. "Where are you?"

Silence answered him.

"Cody. Cody!" Mariana started for the paddock gate.

"I'll find him."

Panic coursed through Jacob, building with each thrum of his pulse. Following his gut, he headed for the dark corners. But his gut failed him. Cody wasn't in any of them.

By now, Mariana was in the paddock. Mindless of her clothes and high heels, she cupped her hands to her mouth and called repeatedly for Cody. "Honey bun, please answer me."

Where did he go? The question resounded inside Jacob's head like an angry tirade. How could he have been so stupid as to forget about his son? Even for a few minutes. There was danger everywhere. Sharp tools in the storage room. Deadly insects like scorpions and bees. He'd seen a rattlesnake in the tack room just last week. Hooves that could trample a small boy.

Hooves!

Jacob ran straight for Amigo's stall. The old horse was gentle, but he weighed fifty times what Cody did. And accidents happened…

"Mariana, hurry!" Jacob stood outside the stall, his chest tight to the point of pain. "I found Cody."

"Daddy!"

"Hey, partner. You scared me." With shaking hands, Jacob pushed the open stall door wider and went inside. How had Cody reached the latch? He'd need to put a lock on that. "What are you doing?"

"Ride Migo."

"It's kind of late for that. How 'bout tomorrow, okay?"

"Okay, Daddy." Cody stood by Amigo's chest, his arms wrapped around the horse's front leg.

Amigo lowered his large head and nuzzled Cody's ski cap. Encountering the fuzzy ball sewn on top, he jerked back and snorted in disgust.

"Come here." Without thinking, Jacob knelt and opened his arms.

Cody let go of Amigo and tumbled into Jacob's embrace. Hugging the boy tight, he rose. An emotion the likes of which he'd never felt before came over him, covering him like a warm blanket. Comforting. Secure. Safe. This emotion, Jacob knew with absolute certainty, would stay with him always, a part of him now. Growing bigger and stronger.

"I love you, son," he said into Cody's ear. "Don't run off again."

Cody drew back to study Jacob's face. With

his two small hands, he patted Jacob's cheeks. "Wuv you."

He didn't know how it was possible, but the entire world changed then. Became a different, brighter, better place. And the empty hole in his heart that had been there since his mother's death shrank.

"Come on, son." He gave Amigo's neck a pat. "Thanks for taking care of him, old boy."

At the door to the stall, he and Cody ran into Mariana. He wasn't feeling himself yet and dreaded the chewing-out she was bound to give him.

She didn't. Not one word. And when he finally found the courage to look her in the eyes, he saw that hers were wet with tears.

Chapter 9

Jacob wasn't used to being off on a weekday. But Darius had called and requested a personal day to attend college orientation with his youngest son. Since he'd recently used all his vacation time, Jacob agreed to switch days with him.

As a result, he'd been puttering around the house all morning. Almost unheard of for him.

Mariana had offered to drop Cody off at day care; they paid by the week whether he went or not. Jacob said no, wanting to spend the day with his son. At the look of concern crossing her face, he'd assured her there would be no repeat of the previous night's near disaster. Cody wouldn't leave his sight for a second.

Jacob occupied a good part of his free time with chores and a few minor repairs. Cody was his constant shadow. At the moment, they were having lunch. Just two guys sitting around the table eating and talking, albeit Jacob did most of the talking.

"What's on your schedule this afternoon?"

"Juice." Cody banged his empty sippy cup on his high chair tray.

Jacob reached over and took the cup, refilling it from the bottle of apple juice. "I was thinking of maybe building a sandbox. Your aunt Mariana probably wouldn't like that. She doesn't understand the relationship a man has with his tools. It's part of our genetic makeup."

"Want cookie."

"Finish your macaroni and cheese first."

Cody banged his tray again, this time with his palm. "Cookie."

Where had this sudden outburst come from? It was still too early for nap time. Was he having one of those terrible twos tantrums Mariana had warned Jacob about?

His cell phone rang. Jacob retrieved it from the counter, noting Carly's number on the display.

"What are you doing?" he asked, one eye on his temperamental son.

"I heard through the grapevine you were off work today."

"Yeah, a schedule change."

"As it happens, I'm off, too. You available for a playdate?"

Jacob tried to recall the last time Carly had spontaneously invited him to do something with her and drew a blank.

The changes he'd felt the past few months with both Carly and Lizzie were continuing. Growing. Becoming commonplace.

Playdate? Sure, why not?

"Count me in. Except no trail riding or going out for a beer. I have Cody with me."

She laughed, an easy, pleasant sound. As if they had always laughed together. Or would from now on.

"Silly. I meant the kids. Long story short, I'm watching Rosie today. I thought maybe you could bring Cody to the Roughneck. Brock had one of those trampolines installed in the backyard."

"Trampoline? Aren't Rosie and Cody too little for that?" Jacob pictured Cody tripping over the chair leg the other day at breakfast. His son was nothing if not a born klutz. He'd break his neck on a trampoline.

"No, no. It's smaller than a regular trampoline and built into the ground so kids can't fall. Well, they can still fall, but they're a lot less likely to get hurt. Really, it's pretty cool. You should see it."

A playdate with Cody and Carly's soon-to-be stepdaughter. Jacob chuckled to himself. His life was changing by the minute.

"Cody usually takes a nap around two."

"So does Rosie. Wait till then, throw him in the car and come over. If he's still asleep when you get here, we'll lay him on the couch."

Jacob had one last question. "Is Brock there?"

"Nope. He's at the office today. A board meeting or something. Thank goodness. He's been such a grump lately."

She'd get no argument from Jacob.

"Savannah's handling the store," Carly continued. "Which frees me to watch Rosie. Come on, Jacob. It'll be fun."

"All right, all right."

He filled the time until two by choosing a location for the sandbox, taking measurements, staking out the area and making a list of materials. They brought Buster along with them. The dog loved visiting the ranch, and Cody was thrilled to have someone sharing the backseat with him. For all of three minutes, which was how long it took for him to fall asleep. Buster, too.

Jacob called Mariana during the drive, telling her about the playdate. He didn't mention the trampoline. If it looked too dangerous, he wouldn't let Cody near it. Period. On impulse—Carly's spontaneity must be contagious—he invited Mariana to the Roughneck after work.

"It'll be fun," he said, echoing Carly.

"You sure I won't be interfering?"

"Absolutely not."

"All right."

He liked the silky tone her voice had taken on. Suddenly, the playdate had new meaning for him.

Jacob's concern about the trampoline was completely unfounded. Cody liked jumping, right up until the moment he face-planted after colliding with Rosie. Other than a small red mark on his nose, he was unhurt. Even so, he wouldn't go near the trampoline again, choosing instead to ride his stick pony around the yard, Buster in hot pursuit.

Jacob thought about telling Cody he should be tougher and man up. Not let a girl best him.

"He'll be fine," Carly said as if reading his mind. "It's still new. Rosie wouldn't go near the trampoline for the first three days."

Eventually, the little girl abandoned jumping in order to play with Cody and Buster. He tried teaching her the "leave it" command. She was more interested in Migo.

Jacob and Carly sat in lawn chairs watching the children. She couldn't stop gushing about Lizzie's new baby.

"You should see her. I can't believe how big she's getting. And she's only a few weeks old."

Jacob thought it interesting that Lizzie would choose to name her daughter Natalie Adele, in part after her missing mother. Missing as in abandoning her children when they were young and never returning. Maybe blood was thicker than water.

Not in Jacob's case. Should he ever have another son, no way in hell was he naming him after his father. A daughter, now that was a different story. He'd happily honor his mother's memory by naming a daughter Margaret. Meg for short. He liked the sound of that.

Whoa! A daughter? Where did that come from? He was hardly used to having a son.

"Have you convinced Mariana to come to Thanksgiving Day dinner?" Carly asked.

"I'm working on it."

"Work harder."

"She's meeting us here after work. You try."

Carly's eyes sparked. "Are you two dating yet?"

He tried not to react. If Carly learned he'd kissed Mariana, twice, her curiosity would know no bounds. "I'm not her type."

"She's staying with you."

"Temporarily. Until Cody adjusts."

"He looks adjusted to me."

Cody had settled in nicely and quickly, especially considering it was his third home in four months.

"He's doing all right."

"Have you and Mariana discussed her moving out?" Carly evidently wasn't giving up.

"No." Jacob hadn't mentioned it and neither had Mariana. Truthfully, he wasn't ready for her to leave. And not because she helped with Cody's care.

He liked seeing her emerge from her bedroom in the early morning as he was leaving for work, wearing that silly robe and her long hair a tangled mess. He liked seeing her come home after work and kick off those high-heeled shoes that had to hurt her feet. He like the way she smelled. The way she tasted. The way she rewarded herself for her hard work with a semi-luxury car, small but expensive jewelry and the occasional designer clothes. The way she went from career woman to doting parent in the blink of an eye.

He'd really liked the way she looked at him last night after hearing him tell Cody he loved him.

Granted, Mariana was different from the women Jacob normally dated. He was willing to try something new. He was less sure of her willingness. Definitely not while she was living with him. Maybe after she moved out. Except he didn't want that.

Lizzie appeared, pushing a stroller. "Savannah said I'd find you here." She parked the stroller next to her sister, who jumped up for a peek at the baby.

Jacob immediately vacated his chair and

offered it to Lizzie, then brought another one back from the patio for himself. Before sitting, he gave the baby a dutiful uncle once-over. "Her face isn't so puckered anymore."

Lizzie punched him in the arm. "She's beautiful."

Actually, for a newborn, little Natalie Adele was kind of cute.

"Just like her mom."

That seemed to mollify his sister.

"Have you asked him yet?" Lizzie's stage whisper was anything but quiet.

"Way to go, big mouth." Carly shot her sister an admonishing look.

"Ask me what?"

"We're in need of a…" Carly hesitated. "A favor of sorts."

"Not from you," Lizzie quickly amended. "Mariana. We're hoping you'll use your influence with her on our behalf."

"What kind of favor?" Jacob made sure Cody and Rosie were all right before turning back to his sisters.

"We'd pay, of course." This from Lizzie. "We wouldn't expect her or her firm to do it for free."

"Ask her when she gets here."

"But will you help us convince her?" Carly pleaded.

Jacob wasn't sure how he felt about imposing on Mariana. "She's pretty busy with this high-profile case. The one against Paulo Molinas and Medallion Investments."

"Please," Lizzie gazed at him with sad puppy dog eyes. "It would mean a lot to us."

His sisters' obvious efforts at coercion were having an effect on him. Weakening his resistance. And while they were imposing on him, he found he didn't mind. Not the way he once might have. "Sure."

"Thank you." Carly slumped with relief.

"What do you want from her?"

"Well, as you know, Travis has been attempting to narrow the search for our mother."

"Jet mentioned something about him learning your mother changed her name."

"Yeah, to Adele Black."

"It seems there are a quite a few Adele Blacks in Texas," Carly said. "Even more of them around the country. It's not easy, and Travis's resources are limited. We were hoping Mariana could use her considerably greater resources at Hasbrough and Colletti."

Jacob stopped her before she could continue. "I know an Adele Black."

Both women stared at him. "You do?" Lizzie asked.

"She's the head of AB Windpower. I met her at an alternative energy symposium last year."

"Oh…my God!" Lizzie sat back, a hand pressed to her chest. "That's the company buying up our stock."

Of course, Jacob had heard about the considerably smaller energy company and its purchase of Baron stock. It wasn't enough to be a threat. Not possible as Brock held the majority share. It was, however, a point of interest with the family and with the Baron board of directors. Perhaps a point of concern.

"I'm calling Travis." Lizzie grabbed her phone. "Have him email you all the info he has."

"This can't be a coincidence," Carly said. "A woman with the same *new* name as our mother owning the company that's buying up Baron stock."

Lizzie moved the phone away from her mouth. "There has to be a connection."

A few minutes later, Jacob's phone chimed. "Let me check this. Make sure everything came through." He opened the email and the attached photos, scrolling quickly through them. "That's her." He enlarged the picture of the Adele Black he'd met and handed his phone to his sisters.

"It's Mom." Lizzie's expression was filled with awe.

Carly studied the screen and appeared less convinced. "It does look a little like her. But this woman is thinner, and her hair is different."

Lizzie nodded confidently. "No doubt about it."

"Let's get Savannah's opinion before we go all crazy. And Jet's."

"He was young when Mom left and probably doesn't remember her much."

Jacob checked on Cody and Rosie while his sisters talked. He could only imagine what they were feeling. Hope. Excitement. Joy. Anger. Betrayal. He was familiar with the last two. In a way, his father had also abandoned his family.

When he returned to his chair, he said, "I'll phone Mariana. See if she can dig up some background on this Adele Black before she gets here."

"Really?" Carly jumped from her chair and kissed Jacob's cheek. "You're a good brother."

Lizzie reached over and squeezed his fingers. "Thank you."

"No problem." He automatically squeezed her fingers in return, then with purpose.

This was the most genuine affection he could recall sharing with his sisters. With any of his Baron siblings. He could, he thought with a smile, get used to it.

Mariana answered his call on the second ring. "Is Cody okay?"

"He's fine.

"No broken bones, no cuts or bruises. He doesn't like the new trampoline."

"Trampoline?"

"Relax. It's not what you think. I'll tell you about it later. In the meantime…"

He proceeded to fill her in on Adele Black and AB Windpower, and that the woman could possibly be Carly's and Lizzie's mother.

"I know it's a lot to ask," Jacob said to Mariana. "You're already busy. The girls say they'll pay. They don't expect you to work for free."

"Tell them not to worry. We have a team of investigators. One of them owes me a favor for helping his wife with an auto insurance claim when she was in an accident."

"That'd be great, Mariana. Thank you."

"I understand their plight. No one should be in the position of searching for their parent."

Was she talking about Cody and her decision to tell Jacob about him, or her mother's situation with her father? Regardless, Jacob was appreciative of her willingness.

Carly nudged him. "Ask her how long it will take."

Jacob lifted the phone away from his face. "She'll get to it when she can."

"I heard that," Marina told him when he returned to their call. "I'll do my best, but tell her she has to be patient. These things can take a while."

"Thanks." He lowered his voice. "See you soon."

Feeling the heat of his sisters stares, he looked up. "What?"

"Just friends," Lizzie snorted. "Isn't that what he said at dinner a few weeks ago?"

"Right." Carly drew out the word. "The last time I talked to a *friend* like that, he was my *boy*friend."

Jacob ignored their giggling, wondering if he shouldn't rethink this getting closer to his siblings. There were definite drawbacks.

At a sharp knock on the front door, Buster started barking. He charged full steam ahead out of the bedroom, skidding as he took the corner.

"Apparently you're not that deaf." Jacob set his shaving case on the bathroom counter and followed the dog at a considerably slower pace.

They weren't expecting anyone, certainly not at seven-thirty at night. He'd been in the process of packing. He and Daniel were leaving bright and early in the morning for Fayetteville, Arkansas, and the All Pro Rodeo. Mariana was giving Cody his bath. This had been their routine the past few Thursday evenings.

As much as Jacob was looking forward to the rodeo and the wins he desperately needed, he hated leaving Mariana and Cody. Hated missing them, and not just because thoughts of them were a distraction.

The knocking resumed, louder this time. Buster sat at the door whining, his tail sweeping the floor. Jacob didn't bother looking through the peephole, figuring it was one of the local kids selling something for their school or a neighbor wanting to borrow a tool. Had he left the sprinkler system out front running again?

"Hold your horses." Flipping on the outside light, he opened the door and silently cursed himself. Peepholes were there for a reason.

Brock stood on the front stoop, tall and steady with the help of his cane.

"Am I interrupting?" He didn't wait for an answer and stepped over the threshold.

Daniel followed on his heels. "Hey, Jacob."

His brother with Brock? That was unexpected and put Jacob immediately on edge. "What are you doing here?"

"I'm the driver."

Another time, Jacob would have laughed at the ludicrousness of the situation. "Is there a problem at the drill site?" He couldn't think of another reason for this unannounced visit.

"Nope." Brock glanced around. "Can we sit? This damn leg's still giving me fits."

"Why not?" Jacob started for the family room.

"Here's fine." Brock groaned as he lowered himself onto the living room couch. "More privacy."

Privacy? Jacob didn't need another lecture.

"I'll take a whiskey if you have it." Brock smiled. "Neat."

"Aren't you still on pain medication?"

"I'm not driving."

"Yeah, what's with that?"

Daniel lifted a shoulder. "He caught me as I was leaving. How could I say no?"

Jacob went to the kitchen and the overhead cabinet where he kept a small supply of liquor. While he was pouring Brock's drink, Mariana appeared, carrying a freshly bathed Cody. The boy's skin shone, and his still-damp hair clung to his head. He wore his favorite Superman pajamas.

"Who's here?" she asked in a hushed voice.

"Brock."

"Why? What's wrong?"

"I don't know. He wants to talk."

"Down, down," Cody squawked and squirmed in Mariana's arms. She set him on the floor.

"Is that my grandson?" Brock hollered from the living room.

Cody spun, then darted in that direction, the vinyl feet of his pajama bottoms making tapping sounds on the tile floor. There was no stopping him, but Jacob hurried after him anyway, the tumbler of whiskey in one hand, a soda for Daniel in the other.

Cody stood still, his gaze going from Brock to Daniel with a mixture of fear and fascination.

"Hey there, young man." Brock perched on the edge of the couch and held out his arms to the boy. "Come over here and give your grandfather a hug."

Jacob drew up short. Strange, he thought. And a little disconcerting. Brock hadn't shown any real interest in Cody since the family dinner when he'd questioned Jacob's ability to balance his job, rodeoing and the demands of fatherhood. From what Carly told him, Brock lavished attention on Lizzie's daughter. His biological grandchild.

With a little coaxing, Cody finally went over to Brock and shook the man's hand. Brock made a big deal of greeting the boy and pulled him into a bear hug.

Jacob waited for Cody to start crying. He was still shy around strangers. Cody fooled him by giggling when Brock finally let go. It was then Jacob realized Brock had been tickling Cody.

Raising six rough-and-tumble children probably did teach a person a thing or two about kids. And Brock, despite all his gruffness and faults, *had* raised his children. Not left them like their mother Adele or Jacob's father. That said something about the man's character.

He'd also adopted Jacob and Daniel. In order to spare them the humiliation of bearing their father's last name and the terrible reputation associated with it.

Had Jacob been too rough on Brock all these years? It was something worth considering at a time when the man in question wasn't sitting ten feet away. Maybe he and Daniel could talk about it during their trip to Fayetteville.

Eventually, Mariana joined them in order to take Cody to bed.

Brock struggled to feet. "Mariana."

"It's all right," she told him. "You don't have to get up."

"I want to apologize for my behavior the other day at dinner. I was out of line. And rude."

Jacob was taken aback. Brock didn't apologize often. He exchanged looks with Daniel, who also appeared surprised.

Mariana, however, was gracious. "Thank you."

Daniel succeeded in getting a high five from Cody. "'Night, partner."

Brock went for another bear hug. "You call me Grandpa, okay?" He tapped his chest with his fingers. "Grandpa."

"Gampa," Cody said.

"That's right." Brock's wrinkled face lit with joy, and he patted Cody's head. "A fine boy you have there," he said when Mariana and Cody had left.

"I agree." Jacob sat in the armchair adjacent to the couch where Brock and Daniel sat.

"Shame about his mother," Brock said.

"It is."

"Carly told me your history with her and how you came to have Cody."

Jacob hadn't said anything to his sister. Luke must have mentioned it. At first, Jacob experienced a surge of resentment at both his friend and sister. They had no business blabbing his personal business. Especially to Brock. Then he decided it didn't matter. Jacob wasn't embarrassed or ashamed, and the story had to come out sometime.

"What is it you want, Brock?"

The older man chuckled. "You're always to the point. I like that about you, son." He hitched a thumb at Daniel. "Your brother here prefers to keep people guessing."

Daniel sat back. So much for being friendly. Whatever was going on here, he wasn't a part of it.

Jacob waited. Brock would say what he wanted in his own good time.

It came a moment later. "Your rankings

have dropped." He expelled a long breath. "I'm concerned."

A lecture. Brock could have spared himself the trip.

"I have two more rodeos between now and Nationals to qualify. I can do it."

"I've always liked your confidence, too. You see something you want, and you go after it." Brock chuckled and slapped his leg. The next moment, he sobered and drew a long breath. "Starr Solar Systems has come up for sale."

Evidently, the rumblings were no longer rumors. "It's official, then."

"I'm having Milt make some inquiries."

The Baron Energies head attorney. Brock must be serious about those inquiries.

"It would be a good investment." Excitement surged inside Jacob. He did his best to temper it.

He'd been after Brock for months, years, to invest in alternative energy. He couldn't imagine Brock making a snap decision. Not without an ulterior motive.

"You didn't come all this way to tell me that."

"If everything looks good, I'll instruct Milt to proceed with the acquisition. Once the purchase is final, I'll put you in charge of transitioning Starr Solar into Baron Energies and running it."

"Congratulations!" Daniel grinned broadly. "I always knew you'd change the old man's mind."

"Old man?" Brock feigned indignation. "Who are you calling old?"

Jacob ignored their levity. He needed a moment to absorb the enormity of what Brock had just presented. This was it. What he'd been working toward his entire career. There was so much to say. Questions. Ideas. Suggestions.

He settled on a simple, "You won't regret it."

"Well, it's not exactly that easy."

"I realize there may be other interested parties—"

"I'm not talking about the purchase. You have to qualify for Nationals first. I'd rather you take home a title, but I'll settle for you going."

"Done." Jacob rose.

"Just like that? You haven't competed particularly well lately."

"I told you. I'm going to Vegas. You can buy your ticket now."

"Good." Brock polished off his whiskey. Setting the empty glass on the side table, he also rose, his legs wobbling slightly before he steadied himself. "Take care of that young cowboy in there. He's a chip off the old block."

"Count on it."

Daniel came over to shake Jacob's hand, his grip firm. "Take care of that pretty gal, too." He winked.

"It's not—"

"Don't bother. You aren't fooling anybody."

Jacob walked them outside. Daniel got in the truck while Jacob opened the passenger door.

Brock paused before climbing in and placed an arm around Jacob's shoulders. "Call me from Fayetteville Sunday evening. Let me know how you did."

It was the closest they'd come to a hug since Jacob was a teenager.

Chapter 10

Jacob found Mariana in the kitchen, fixing herself a cup of herbal tea. It was a frequent nighttime ritual for her. She'd also changed for bed and was wearing that thick robe she liked so much.

"Cody asleep?" he asked.

"Out like a light."

"Good. I thought the excitement from Brock's visit might keep him awake."

"By the way, I'm driving to Amarillo on Sunday." She grimaced. "That almost sounds like the lyrics to a George Strait song."

"You listen to country music?"

"I am from Texas."

"But do you like it?"

She wagged a warning finger at him. "If you ever tell anyone, I'll deny it and accuse you of hearsay."

They both laughed at that.

"I called Simone. She can watch Cody until you return from Fayetteville." After a pause, Mariana added, "You were right to hire her."

Jacob put a cupped hand to his ear. "Can you repeat that?"

"Once was hard enough to choke out, thank you very much."

"I promise not to gloat."

She searched his face. "You're happy."

It must show. "Baron Energies is purchasing Starr Solar Systems. Brock is turning it over to me to run."

"That's wonderful!"

"Well, there is a condition."

"Hmm. Brock. Condition. You can't be surprised."

"I have to qualify for Nationals."

She lifted the tea bag from the cup and squeezed the last drops from it. "Can you?"

"I told Brock to consider it a done deal."

Interest flickered in her eyes. "Does this mean a desk job's in your future?"

"Eventually. I'll have to spend some time

at Starr's headquarters. More early on until the transition's complete. They're located in northeast Dallas."

"Oh." Like that, the interest dimmed. "You'll have an even longer commute."

"Temporarily. You don't need to worry about Cody."

"Can't help it. I always will."

"Between me, the nanny and you, we'll work things out."

"Remember, I won't be here that much longer."

Jacob moved closer to her. "You don't have to move out."

"I'm not sure postponing is wise."

"You want to leave Cody?"

"Of course not. But we can't continue to live indefinitely as housemates."

Because their feelings for each other went well beyond platonic. She didn't have to say it. Jacob could read it in her expression. Hear it in her voice.

"Unless we modify the arrangement."

"We've had this conversation before. Nothing's changed."

"Everything has. Brock is purchasing Starr Solar Systems."

"You and I dating will confuse Cody."

"How? I'm his father, and he thinks you're his mother. He'll be more confused by us not dating."

Mariana shook her head and reestablished the distance between them. "You're attracted to me is all."

"Not true." He realized his mistake the moment the words were out. "I mean, I'm more than attracted to you. I care. A lot."

"Are you sure? We're living together. Like a family. Taking care of Cody together. Sharing the chores. The arrangement's creating an artificial closeness."

"There's nothing artificial about my feelings for you." He reached up and rubbed the back of his knuckles along the line of her jaw. He might have kissed her if she didn't turn away.

"Which complicates things that much more."

"What's really wrong, Mariana?"

"You may be sure about your feelings for me, but I'm not."

She was afraid that the connection they'd formed wasn't real. He had to convince her differently.

"When we kiss, those sparks, they're real."

She sighed and took a sip of her tea.

"I understand your reservations," he said.

"That's good. But I also need you to respect them."

She gazed up at him and pain reflected in her eyes. Had she been hurt before? By someone other than her father?

"I won't be rodeoing after next month. I'm getting too old."

"Brock's continuing to compete, and he's seventy."

"He's retired now."

"Only because he was injured."

"I'm not like him."

She abruptly opened the cabinet door beneath the sink and disposed of her tea bag in the trash bin. "You're a lot more like him than you care to admit."

"Are you comparing me to Brock or your father? There's a difference."

"Between them?" She straightened.

"Between me and either of them. I'm committed to being a good father to Cody."

"And me being here with you makes that easier. You rely on me to pick up the slack."

Jacob's first reaction was to be insulted. Then, he reconsidered. There was a measure of truth to her concerns.

He took her arm and gently turned her toward him. "You like me. I know you do. More than like me."

"Jacob."

"Give me, this, us, a chance."

"I don't want to be hurt. Worse, I don't want Cody to be hurt. There's too much at stake. What if we start seeing each other and, after a while, break up? He'll be heartbroken."

Jacob wished he could say the right thing to erase her concerns. He opted to let his actions speak for him.

Bending his head, he kissed her. Lightly at first, then with increased pressure. For her part, she held back, the hands she placed on his chest resisting rather than caressing.

"I'm not like them," he repeated softly against her lips.

"Promise?"

"Let me prove it."

His lips wandered her face, stopping at her temples, the center of her forehead, each cheek and the corners of her mouth. She shivered when he trailed kisses down the side of her neck, then back up to claim her mouth again.

A soft moan emanated from low in her throat. Was it one of surrender? He hoped so. Sliding his palms up the sides of her rib cage, he stopped just beneath her breasts. She went still.

Jacob went no further. This wasn't what he wanted, her thinking his sweet talk and kisses were only a means to get her into bed. And she might well think that.

As a result, it was him and not her who pulled back and broke off the kiss. "Good night, Mariana."

A brief flash of indecision clouded her features. A second later, it cleared. "Good night, Jacob. See you in the morning."

He didn't go to bed. Not straightaway. He went to his home office in the third bedroom and powered up his laptop. There was no new information to be found on the sale of Starr Solar Systems. He answered a few emails and checked his bank account balances. The ringing of his cell phone interrupted him. It was Daniel.

"You still up?" he asked.

"Just heading to bed."

"I won't take long. Jet called. He's not going with us to Fayetteville."

Jacob had seen this coming, what with Jet's priorities changing. "Guess it'll be just you and me."

"Or we can stay home," Daniel suggested.

"Not a chance. Not me, anyway."

"I was kidding."

"What do you think of Brock's offer?" Jacob asked.

"He's serious."

"But knowing him, there's an ulterior motive."

"He did talk to me about my future on the ride over."

"Was that why he coerced you into driving him?"

"Probably." Daniel chuckled. "Or he wanted a reliable witness when he talked to you."

"See you in the morning, brother."

It was only after he hung up that it occurred to Jacob he did sound a lot like Brock and, possibly, Mariana's father, Zeb Snow. No wonder she had her doubts about him and his intentions. In her shoes, he'd feel the same way.

Jacob straddled the bucking chute and settled himself in place, ready to spot his brother. Beside him, Daniel climbed the chute. It was his turn to compete, and he'd drawn the toughest bull at the All Pro Rodeo. Living up to his reputation, Rocket Man swung his massive head side to side, banging his horns into the metal sides.

"You got this, bro," Jacob assured Daniel. "You've ridden him before."

Daniel had. Last year. And taken home third place. He would, he'd boasted earlier, do better today.

Sunday afternoon, the final round of bull riding, the last event of the rodeo. Both Jacob and Daniel would be taking home buckles. Jacob had finished second in saddle bronc riding, and Daniel third. Daniel had also taken third in steer wrestling. If he did well riding Rocket Man, he'd beat out Jacob who, at this moment, held first place.

Only one competitor remained left after Daniel, and he wasn't a threat. Regardless of how Daniel performed, Jacob was in the money and one step closer to qualifying for Nationals.

He'd been right to tell Brock to buy his plane ticket for Vegas. Jacob was going; he could feel it in his bones. He'd been in the zone all weekend. Sure, he'd thought of Cody and Mariana. But he was able to put thoughts of them aside when his number was called.

A smile tugged at his mouth. He was getting the hang of this delicate balancing act. When he went to Nationals in a few weeks, he'd go confident he could win. Though he'd have earned the real prize before stepping on that plane. Starr Solar Systems.

And as promised, he'd retire from rodeoing after Nationals. Mariana would see that he was serious, about being a good father to Cody and about her.

"Easy does it." Jacob kept a close watch as Daniel slowly lowered himself onto the bull's back and took hold of the flat braided rope.

Rocket Man humped his back in anticipation, already attempting to unseat Daniel before the chute door was even open. For a harrowing few seconds, Daniel's knee remained pinned between the bull's side and the chute wall. Just as suddenly, the bull eased up.

Daniel groaned.

Jacob laid a steadying hand on his brother's back. "You okay?"

"Right as rain."

It would take a lot more than a pinned knee to deter Daniel. He was just as intent on winning as Jacob had been.

Another test of the rope's tightness, one last tug on the brim of his hat, and Daniel was ready. "Go," he said and nodded.

The chute door flew open. Rocket Man was instantly in motion, hell-bent on getting this nuisance off his back. Daniel hung on, effortlessly riding the bull's twists, turns and relentless bucking. No sooner did he raise his legs to spur the bull's shoulders than Rocket Man launched himself in the opposite direction.

Jacob risked a glance at the clock: 6.8 seconds. Almost there.

"Come on, Danny boy. You got this."

Jacob wanted the gold. He'd settle for silver if it meant losing to his brother.

All at once, Rocket Man jumped, high enough that all four hooves were off the ground, and flung his huge body sideways. Daniel managed to tuck his body into a semi-ball before hitting the ground like a ton of bricks at the exact moment the buzzer sounded. The crowd groaned in unison.

Jacob waited. He wasn't worried. Not at first. Falling, being thrown, was part and parcel of bull riding. He'd certainly taken his share of knocks and lived to tell about it.

Only Daniel didn't rise, and the seconds ticked by. Five of them.

Jacob leaped off the chute wall. The bullfighters were frantically distracting Rocket Man, attempting to keep him away from Daniel and headed down the arena toward the exit gate. Bulls could and would go after a fallen cowboy.

Reaching the arena fence, Jacob started to scale it. He didn't get far.

"Hold on, partner." A cowboy grabbed him by the right arm.

A second one latched on to his left. "Wait till the coast is clear."

Daniel still hadn't moved. Jacob's heart punched repeatedly into his sternum with relentless thrusts. A roar filled his ears. "That's my brother in there."

"Let the bullfighters do their job."

A few seconds later—God, it felt like hours—Rocket Man was trotting through the exit gate and Jacob was hurdling over the arena fence. The heavy dirt pulled at his boots as he ran, slowing him down.

Two of the bullfighters were already at Daniel's side when Jacob finally got there. Other cowboys also came. Jacob didn't count how many. He saw only Daniel.

"You okay?" someone asked.

Daniel stirred. That was a good sign, right? He groaned—also a good sign. Jacob knelt by his brother's side. "Don't move."

"What hurts?" someone else asked.

Daniel grunted through clenched teeth. "My entire left side."

The EMTs on duty arrived. "Clear the way," the taller of the two ordered, and the cowboys surrounding Daniel melted away to give the young men room.

Except for Jacob. "He's my brother," he said and stayed put.

The EMTs took less than thirty seconds to examine Daniel and assess the extent of his injuries. "You're going for a ride, my friend."

The ambulance drove right into the arena. It seemed as if the entire crowd fidgeted nervously while the EMTs stabilized Daniel for transport and took his medical history, then loaded him onto the gurney.

He reached an arm out to Jacob. "Come with me."

Jacob didn't hesitate. He knew his brother's aversion to hospitals. It was something he'd developed after their mother's unexpected death. The staph infection that took her life could only have been contracted in the hospital. Jacob wasn't sure if Daniel's aversion was a fear of dying or simply that hospitals reminded him of their tragic loss.

The ride went quickly, much of it a blur to Jacob. He sat across from Daniel and watched him like a hawk as the EMTs monitored him and communicated via radio with the hospital, informing them of Daniel's condition.

Once there, he was whisked away by a medical team. Jacob was instructed to cool his heels in a family waiting area. He didn't "cool" very well. He expended his nervous energy by pacing and making phone calls to the family. They were upset. Offered to come. Jacob convinced them to wait until he had more news. While Daniel's condition was serious, it didn't appear to be life-threatening.

Wasn't that what the doctors had said about their mother, right up until she caught that infection?

Mariana was last on his call list. She was still in Amarillo, meeting with her client.

"Are you doing all right?" The concern in her voice came through clearly despite their poor connection.

"I'm fine. Not sure when I'll be home."

"You need anything?"

It was nice of her to ask. "Just get home and take care of our son. Simone's had a long day."

"*Our* son?"

"He does call you Mama."

"See you soon."

He swore he could hear her smiling.

Eventually, the doctor appeared to consult with Jacob. The news was good and bad.

"Your brother's a lucky man," the doctor said. "No internal injuries."

The tension Jacob had been holding inside since watching his brother fall left him in a rush.

"The contusions, sprains and soft tissue damage will heal without a problem. He has four fractured ribs and he's torn the ligaments in his right shoulder." The doctor used his hands to show Jacob where on Daniel's body the injuries were located.

"Are you going to operate?"

"No. We'll tape the ribs and shoulder and put him in a sling. He needs to see an orthopedic specialist when he gets home. Right away," the doctor emphasized, then went on to explain the course of treatment.

"When can he leave?"

"We'd like to keep him overnight for observation."

"Can I see him?"

"Of course. He's being moved now to a room. Don't expect much conversation. He's been given a healthy dose of pain medication and will likely sleep through the night."

"I won't stay too long."

While he waited for the nurse to inform him of Daniel's room number, he called the family and updated them on the latest. Brock was already making arrangements for Jet to fly him to Elk City in the morning and retrieve Daniel.

"No need for you to stay," he told Jacob.

"I don't mind."

"I'll be there before he wakes up. You go on, see that son of yours and get some rest. You must be exhausted."

Jacob was. The emotional strain had taken more out of him than the physical one. "Thanks, Brock. Daniel will feel better knowing he's getting out of the hospital right away."

Jacob obeyed the doctor's orders and kept his visit with his brother brief. Just long enough to assure himself Daniel was all right. At least, he would be all right after possible shoulder surgery and months of physical therapy.

Heading toward the exit, he debated between calling a friend or taxi service for a ride back to the rodeo grounds or getting a room at a nearby hotel and meeting Brock in the morning.

Except all he wanted was to go home and

see Mariana and Cody. The need was an ache lodged deep inside his chest.

As if his thoughts had conjured her, she appeared before him, walking briskly through the hospital's large double doors.

Grinding to a halt, he stared, surprised and enormously pleased. Without thinking about it, he pulled her into a fierce hug. "What are you doing here? Amarillo is two hours away."

"I was worried. You sounded bad on the phone. How's Daniel?"

"Resting." He released her. Reluctantly. She'd driven all this way just because he'd sounded bad on the phone. "For now."

"Tell me the details in the car."

"Car?"

"I came here to drive you home."

She'd done that for him? Jacob tried to speak but found the emotions of the past several hours catching up with him and making speech difficult.

"Okay," he finally managed.

Talking about the accident drained him even further. Thirty minutes into the ride, Jacob leaned his seat back and closed his eyes. The last thing he remembered was Mariana reaching over and squeezing his hand.

Chapter 11

"Jacob, we're here."

At the sound of Mariana's voice, he roused himself. They were home, parked in the driveway next to the nanny's car. A glance at the clock on the Infiniti's dash told him better than ninety minutes had come and gone. He must have been tired. Normally, he couldn't sleep in moving vehicles.

"Okay, okay." He sat up and shoved his fingers through his hair, realizing his hat wasn't on his head. It had fallen into the backseat. He reached behind him and retrieved it.

They walked side by side up to the house. This time, she was the one who put a hand in the center of his back to steady him. An overjoyed Buster greeted them as if they'd been gone a month.

While Mariana spoke to Simone—Cody was fast asleep and had been an angel all day—Jacob took Buster outside and called the hospital. The nurse on duty assured him Daniel was resting as comfortably as possible. Next, he listened to his voice mail messages. Evidently his phone had gone off a few times while he'd slept. The last message was from Brock, confirming that he and Jet would be at the hospital by 7:00 a.m.

"Thank goodness she was willing to stay late," he said when Simone had left. "I'm not sure what we'd do without her."

"I know." Mariana stood in the hall. Lifting her long auburn hair with one hand, she rubbed the back of her neck with the other.

Did she have any idea how incredibly sexy she looked? Jacob had to turn away, afraid the desire coursing through him was reflected in his eyes.

"You should go to bed."

His head snapped around at her remark. For a moment, he thought she'd said something entirely different.

This had to stop or he'd drive himself crazy.

"Don't you have to be up early?" he asked.

"Yeah." She shook her loose hair, also incredibly sexy. "See you in the morning."

It *almost* sounded as if she didn't want to retire yet. That, or his imagination was working overtime.

Jacob had to get out of there. Before he did something he shouldn't. Like take her in his arms, then take her to bed. "Thanks again for coming to get me. It meant a lot."

She smiled shyly. "I'd like to think we're friends."

He probably shouldn't say it, but he did. "I'd like to think we're more than friends."

"We are. We're parenting our son together."

"Right." What had he expected? For her to throw herself at him? Not Mariana. Even if she was experiencing the same feelings as him, which he truly believed, she wasn't a throw-herself-at-a-guy kind of gal. "'Night."

Jacob didn't head straight to bed. His lengthy snooze on the ride home had taken the edge off his exhaustion. Instead, he hit the shower, the hot water soothing his aching muscles. Even then, sleep eluded him.

He worried about Daniel and the long road to recovery his brother faced. He thought about Brock and the generous offer to pick up Daniel and fly him home. That was something a father would do for his son and the first selfless gesture Brock had made to either Jacob or Daniel in a long, long while. Jacob also thought about Starr Solar Systems. His buddy Keith had texted earlier and let Jacob know he'd won the gold buckle in bull riding.

That left one more rodeo, one more weekend, and Jacob's dream would become a reality.

Mostly, he thought about Mariana. She'd reiterated on numerous occasions that he wasn't her type. That she didn't trust him or his attraction to her, convinced he was confusing their comfortable living arrangement with affection.

A noise from across the hall had him jerking upright in bed. Cody was awake and crying. Within seconds, Mariana could be heard comforting him. Jacob swung his feet onto the floor and grabbed a pair of sweatpants to cover his boxer briefs. By the time he reached the hall, Buster on his heels, Mariana had taken Cody into the family room.

"Is something wrong?" he asked.

"I don't think so." She balanced Cody on her lap and stroked his hair. "He just woke up crying. His diaper was wet. That might have been the reason." She pressed the back of her hand against his forehead. "He doesn't seem to have a fever."

Jacob went into the kitchen and heated some milk in the microwave. Pouring it into one of Cody's sippy cups, he took the milk to Mariana.

"Try this. My mom used to give me and Daniel warm milk when we were little. She swore by it."

Though Jacob had been careful when heating the milk, Mariana tested the temperature anyway. Cody eagerly accepted the cup and drank lustily.

"Maybe he was just thirsty." She studied him. "This parenting stuff has a pretty steep learning curve."

"You'll get the hang of it. We both will." Jacob sat beside her. "Just takes practice."

"I'll have that, won't I? More practice." She gazed worriedly at him.

"Why wouldn't you?"

"I'm moving out soon."

"Don't remind me."

She returned her attention to Cody, brushing the hair from his face. He was nearly done with the milk and already his eyelids were drooping.

"The case is heating up. Molinas's attorneys have made a settlement offer. It's appallingly low, naturally. But they've so far refused to consider settling, so this is a step in the right direction. My boss is expecting everyone on the team to put in whatever hours are necessary. I'd rather not uproot again if I can help it."

Work, and her possible promotion, was the only reason she'd consider remaining here. Not him. Jacob kept his disappointment to himself. "Then don't uproot yourself. Stay as long as you like."

It might have been the milk, or the sound of his parents talking in murmurs, but a minute later Cody had drifted off.

"I'll put him to bed." Mariana stood. Cody made small sounds of protest at being disturbed but didn't wake.

Jacob waited in the doorway to her room and watched her lay Cody in his crib. The glow from a teddy bear night-light was the only illumination. It softened Mariana's features, turning her from pretty to beautiful.

She caught him staring at her. "What's wrong?"

"Nothing. Simply enjoying the view."

He hadn't intended to be so direct. Neither did he regret it.

She touched her hair self-consciously. "I'm a mess. It's been a long day."

"You always look great."

Giving Cody's back a last tender pat, she stepped away from the crib. "Even though you're lying, I'll say thank you."

"When I was at the hospital today with Daniel, once I knew he was going to be all right, all I could think about was coming home. To Cody, but also to you. You're not just my houseguest, Mariana. You're not just my son's aunt. You're the woman who drives me crazy with the delicious way she smells and the lush, sexy mouth I can't stop thinking about."

"Jacob." She walked slowly toward him. Not, however, to fall into his embrace. Her hand reached for the door as if to close it.

"I want you." Because he couldn't stop himself, he sifted his fingers through her silky hair. The sensation was akin to being struck by lightning. He bent his head.

"Don't," she whispered.

"Why?"

"Because if I let you kiss me, it won't stop there."

"I can behave myself."

"Maybe I can't."

His heart pounded inside his chest. "If you

really feel like that, then how can kissing you possibly be wrong?"

"I didn't say it was wrong. But it may not be smart."

He lowered his head until capturing her mouth was merely a breath away. "Could also be the smartest thing either of us has ever done."

"I'm afraid, Jacob. My father made my mother miserable."

And there it was, what lay at the heart of her reluctance.

"Can I ask you something?"

"What?"

"Are you afraid of ending up like your mother? Or are you afraid of being happy?"

Her eyes widened. "Don't be ridiculous."

"You've been hurt. By your father or someone else. Maybe you think you aren't entitled to happiness because your sister died."

She turned away.

He took hold of her arm, brought her back to him. "Mariana, take a chance with me. You won't be sorry." He dipped his head and let his lips brush ever so lightly across hers.

When he pulled back, she withdrew. Not much. But enough to let him know her answer.

"I'm sorry," she said.

He wouldn't push. Wouldn't force her into

something she wasn't ready for or didn't want. He'd opened his heart to her, assured her his feelings were genuine. That he wouldn't be rodeoing much longer and wouldn't hurt her. There was nothing more he could do.

"All right." Jacob retreated. "Guess I'll see you in the morning."

Closing the door to his room, he shut off the light and started for the bed. He'd just reached the footboard when the knob suddenly turned and the door swung wide.

Mariana stood in the opening, the dim outline of her silhouette recognizable in the darkness.

Jacob knew her. He'd always know her. In the span of a few weeks, she'd become vital to him. So much so that losing her would be worse than losing a limb.

She glided silently across the carpeted floor, untying her robe as she did. "I'm an emotional wreck. I have my parents to thank for that."

Jacob didn't move a muscle, not trusting his legs to support him. "I understand. My dad and Brock have both done a number on me."

She slipped the robe from her shoulders. It puddled at her feet. She wore the sheerest of nighties, the wisp of material barely concealing her. Beneath it, he could just make out the shape of her full breasts and the curve of her hips. Sweat broke out on his forehead, and his lungs labored to draw a decent breath in the suddenly airless room.

"What changed your mind?" he asked.

"As afraid as I am of being hurt, I'm more afraid of not having this night with you and regretting it for the rest of my life."

She met him in the center of the room, a vision come to life.

"I need you to be sure." It required incredible restraint not to reach for her. "Because once we start, there's no going back."

"I'm not sure. I'm taking a leap of faith."

That was good enough for him. Jacob opened his arms. She went into them and, to his surprise and delight, initiated their kiss. His blood instantly heated, and he took the kiss from hot to smoldering.

She put up no resistance when his tongue sought entrance to her mouth. If anything, she encouraged him by winding her arms around his neck and pressing herself against him. They stumbled to the bed, with Jacob yanking down his sweatpants along the way. At the side of the bed, he managed to step out of them, all without tripping or breaking off their kiss.

His efforts were for nothing. Placing her palms on his chest, she pushed him away.

"Wait." Standing before him, she lifted the hem of her nightie. A moment later, it fluttered to the floor, landing beside her robe.

Jacob stared. She was a sight, and he wished he could see more of her. To compensate for the lack of light, he used his hands, filling them with the plump softness of her breasts and learning their shape. Her nipples rose to taut peaks as his thumbs grazed them.

She sighed contentedly, then moaned with pleasure when he lowered his head to take one ripe nipple in his mouth.

"Please," she murmured.

"Anything, sweetheart. What do you want?"

"This." Hooking her thumbs into the waistband of his boxer briefs, she slid them down over his hips. He kicked off the briefs, leaving them both naked.

No. Wrong. Only him. She still wore a pair of panties, if the thin strip of see-through material could be called that. She started to remove them.

"Let me," he said and did just that. Slowly, in order to savor every moment. Her legs, gorgeous in skirts, were spectacular when bared.

He glanced up to see her watching him, and

the intense jolt of desire racing through him nearly knocked him sideways. He wanted to take her right there and then, might have if the last shred of common sense remaining wasn't shouting loud and clear.

"I have protection. In the nightstand. I haven't needed it for a while—"

"Shut up." She rose on tiptoes and kissed him hungrily. "It's enough you have it. The details aren't important."

How had he gotten so incredibly lucky to have met a woman like her?

Laying her on the bed, he covered her with his body. They fit perfectly. More so when he nudged her legs apart and settled himself in the warm junction of her legs.

"I'm going to make love to you, Mariana."

She laughed softly. It was like music. "I certainly hope so, or all my efforts at seduction were wasted."

"Not wasted at all. But I need to tell you, this won't be just sex for me. I care about you. A lot."

She met his gaze and held it. "I wouldn't be here if I doubted that."

"Good." He moved his hips, pressing his erection solidly against her belly.

She arched her back in response, meeting his thrusts. This was going to be very, very good.

"Not so fast," he said into the side of her neck where he'd been nibbling her delicate skin. There was the matter of the condom. He levered up on his elbows, leaned over and removed one from the nightstand drawer.

"Aren't you going to put it on?" she asked when he began working his way down her body, touching and tasting and nuzzling every incredible inch of her.

"First, I'm going to make you glad you took that walk across the hall to my room."

Jacob delivered on his promise. Mariana made it easy. She was incredibly responsive, encouraging him with breathy words and languid sighs, and even going so far as to take his hand and placing it where she wanted to be touched. That excited him. She excited him. Her climax, when it came, nearly caused him to lose control.

"I want you, too," she murmured, a desperate quality in her voice. "Inside me."

Jacob was only too happy to oblige. Tearing open the condom, he quickly took care of business, never taking his eyes off Mariana. He'd barely finished when she sat up, pushed him onto his back and straddled his middle.

"Like this." She took him in her hands and guided him inside her.

For a moment, he couldn't move. Couldn't breathe. Couldn't think. Couldn't remember his own name. Then she started rocking her hips, and Jacob was lost to everything but her.

She leaned down, bringing her mouth to his. "Kiss me."

He hooked an arm around her neck, another around her waist. Anchoring her to him, he did as she asked while thrusting deeper and faster. She groaned and tensed. The thrill of hearing her call his name was all it took for Jacob to find his own release.

"You're incredible," he said when he could talk again.

"You're not so bad yourself." Smiling, she eased off of him and stretched out beside him, an arm draped over his waist, her legs tangled with his.

"You cold?" he asked, pulling her closer.

"A little."

He drew the bedcover over the two of them. Skin to skin, alone in the darkened house except for a sleeping Cody, was like being the sole inhabitants of their own private world. Jacob thought he could grow used to it.

Mariana's confidence must have deserted her, because she asked, "What now?"

"You call the shots. We move fast or slow, whatever speed you're comfortable with."

"Do we sleep together every night?"

"Only if you want." He desperately hoped she did.

"Sounds an awful lot like playing house."

"This isn't playing house for me. I've never been more serious."

"What about Cody?"

"He's old enough to sleep by himself, isn't he?"

"That's not what I was talking about."

"I don't think he'll mind. He's two."

She smiled, but even in the dark, he could tell it lacked luster. "He's the most important thing to me in the world. If it comes down to choosing between you and him—"

"It won't come down to that." Jacob kissed her lightly. "I swear. He's the most important thing in the world to me, too."

"What if you get injured like your brother or Brock?"

"I have two more rodeos left, including Nationals. The odds are in my favor I'll walk away unscathed. And with a new job." Jacob rolled her onto her back and trapped her between him and the mattress "Then, I'm officially retiring. Less than a month. Tell me you can live with that."

"I can." She moved beneath him and traced the length of his spine with her fingertips.

"It's all going to work out, sweetheart."

"I hope you're right."

"Count on it."

Mariana may still have had her doubts. Jacob, however, could see their future clear as a bell. It was going to happen—they'd be together. Nothing was standing in their way.

Chapter 12

The past two days were the best Jacob could remember in a long time. He and Mariana were a couple.

Unofficial couple. She'd been crystal clear on that. She didn't want to say anything until after the National Finals Rodeo in December.

Jacob went along with her for the most part. She didn't want people—his family, let's be honest—jumping to the wrong conclusion. That she was with him only because she didn't want to lose shared custody of Cody.

Of course, nothing could be further from the truth. Her feelings for Jacob were real and true, as were his for her. The small doubts that surfaced now and then were simply left-overs from when his father betrayed him and Brock disappointed him.

She also, he supposed, didn't fully trust him. That bothered Jacob the most. He was a man of his word. He would not be competing again after Nationals. She had to believe him.

"Morning!" Simone smiled brightly when he opened the front door.

"How are you doing?"

"I brought some construction paper, glue and crayons." She held up her arm, laden with supplies. Slung over her shoulder was a small canvas tote. Items she'd need for spending the night.

Mariana was off to Houston to attend a deposition with several of Paulo Molinas's former employees and wouldn't be back until the following day. Jacob was heading to the Valle del Sol Rodeo.

"I thought we'd make paper turkeys. For Thanksgiving," Simone explained. "You are having dinner?" She looked momentarily stricken. "Did I make a wrong assumption?"

"Not at all," Jacob assured her. "Paper turkeys are a great idea."

She expelled a relieved sigh and entered

the house. "No scissors, I promise. I precut all the pieces last night."

Jacob again commended himself for making the right decision in hiring Simone. She might not be the most outgoing person in the world, but she was sweet and patient and good with both Cody and Buster, who'd beaten Jacob to the front door to welcome her.

"Mone!" Cody came charging into the living room, calling out his nickname for Simone. Body slamming her right leg, he hugged it. With affection, not fear.

"How's my boy today?"

"Good," Cody shouted.

"Shh. Inside voice, okay?" She handed him her canvas tote. "Can you put this in the bedroom for me?"

He set off, half carrying, mostly dragging his load. By prearranged agreement, Simone was staying in the guest bedroom where Cody slept. Where Mariana *used* to sleep. If Simone thought anything of the new arrangements, she kept it to herself.

Jacob returned to the kitchen for a second cup of coffee. Mariana was still in the bedroom, finishing packing for her trip. She was scheduled to meet the rest of her team in Houston. Jacob didn't have to leave for another two hours. He should pull onto the Valle del Sol Rodeo grounds with plenty of time to spare.

He was feeling good. Psyched. He didn't have to win any events this weekend, only place in the top six spots. That didn't mean he'd settle for less than his best. He could— *would*—do this. For his, Cody's and Mariana's futures.

Just as he was topping off his coffee mug, his cell phone went off, the chime identifying the caller as Daniel.

"Good luck this weekend, bro."

"How you feeling?"

"Like I've been hit by a truck." Daniel was recuperating at the Roughneck. Their sisters had gone from caring for Brock to caring for him.

"Or thrown from a bull?"

"That'll teach me." The threat was a weak one. Jacob suspected his brother would compete again. He didn't have a woman and son waiting at home for him. Too bad.

"Everything still on schedule for Tuesday?" Jacob had agreed to drive his brother to the surgery center and stay with him during the procedure to repair the torn ligaments in his shoulder. While not a hospital, the out-patient facility was enough like a hospital to unnerve Daniel.

"7:00 a.m. sharp. Just so you know, Brock is coming, too."

"Only Brock?"

Daniel laughed. "Funny."

Not really. The Baron family had a habit of showing up in droves.

"I don't mind if that's what you're asking." Between the purchase of Starr Solar Systems and transporting Daniel home after the accident, Jacob's feelings for and patience with his adoptive father had grown.

"I just want this over with."

Jacob could hear the tension in his brother's voice. "From what your doctor says, your recovery is going to be a whole lot worse than the operation itself. I hear physical therapy is a bitch."

"As long as I'm out of that place in the six hours the surgeon promised, I'm okay."

Mariana entered the kitchen, looking killer gorgeous in one of her suits.

"Gotta go," Jacob said. "I'll call you later. Let you know how I did."

He didn't care that Simone was in the house. He hauled Mariana against him for a kiss, which he intended to be brief and wasn't.

When he finally set her on her feet, she was flushed and breathless. "We're not alone," she warned.

A shame, indeed. "Knock 'em dead at the deposition."

"It's really a formality. I don't expect any startling revelations, though it would be nice. I'm not sure why I have to go. Four attorneys seems excessive."

"When did you stop wanting that promotion to junior partner?"

"You're right." She tugged on her jacket lapels. "Duty calls, and I respond."

He fixed her a travel mug of coffee for the road while she went into the family room and said goodbye to Cody. Watching them over the length of the breakfast bar, something inside Jacob shifted. It was his heart continuing to heal.

She sauntered up to him, a smile on her face. "Walk me to my car."

He did and resumed kissing her outside. Though now, instead of Simone, they had curious neighbors to worry about. Actually,

Jacob didn't care who saw them. This was what couples did, unofficial or not.

"Good luck," she said, giving him one last hug.

"You mean that?" He stared down into her eyes.

"I want you to final. What's important to you is important to me."

Another round of goodbyes, and she was in her car and on the road. Jacob felt the loss keenly. Returning to the house, he checked on Cody, then started packing his own bag. An hour later, he was loading the truck.

Simone burst into the garage, her eyes wide with alarm and a whimpering Cody in her arms. "Jacob, I'm sorry to bother you. Something's happened."

"What's wrong?" He charged around the side of the truck. Cody looked fine, but still… "Is he hurt?

"No, no. Not Cody. My daughter's been in an accident. The other driver ran a red light and T-boned her car."

"Is she all right?"

"Yes. No. The air bag went off. Broke her glasses and cut her face. And her knee hit the dash." Simone started to cry. "She's scared."

Jacob placed a hand on her shoulder and squeezed. "What do you need from me?"

She didn't hesitate and passed Cody to him like he was a sack of groceries. "I have to go."

"Sure."

Perhaps because he could sense his nanny's distress, Cody's whimpering escalated into full-fledged squalling.

"Sorry to leave you like this," Simone said over her shoulder.

"No worries." Jacob followed her into the house. "It's your daughter."

He imagined Cody at eighteen, a college freshman on the way to class and being struck by another car. The thought terrified him. Naturally, Simone wanted to rush to her daughter's side.

"Keep me posted," he said.

"Thank you." She fetched her things from the spare bedroom. A minute later, she was flying out the front door.

"Bye-bye." Cody waved between sobs.

Only then Jacob realized he was alone in the house with Cody, needing to leave for the rodeo soon, and that he had no responsible babysitter until Mariana returned tomorrow.

Leeza was the first name that came to mind. Jacob instantly dismissed her. Too much responsibility for a girl her age and too much of an imposition to her parents. His sisters! Wait, not Lizzie. She had a newborn to watch and was chronically exhausted. Savannah and Carly were working in the store. Even so, he tried them.

"How goes it?"

"Not well." Carly sounded stressed. "We're having equipment failure. The walk-in refrigerator is down. The repairman's here now."

"That's good."

"Not good. He's saying the entire motor needs replacing. Naturally, there isn't one in stock, and it'll take a full day to have one delivered. Savannah and I are unloading all the perishables. It's just crazy."

Jacob imagined the monumental task. "I'll let you go."

"Wait a second. You didn't say why you called."

"The nanny's daughter was in a car wreck."

"My God! Is she okay?"

"Minor injuries. She should be all right."

"Can I help? Do you need something?"

"No. You get back to the fridge." He couldn't ask his sisters to watch a toddler on top of everything else they were dealing with.

"Call you later." She hung up an instant later.

Though it was a long shot, Jacob tried Luke next. He had the most experience with two-year-olds. After six rings, the call went to voice mail. Jacob didn't bother with a message.

Desperate, he debated calling Mariana and asking her to turn around. She'd mentioned there were four attorneys and that she wasn't really needed.

No. The promotion was a priority. As was the case. Her clients were depending on her.

One choice remained. Well, two. Jacob could stay home, which wasn't a choice at all as far as he was concerned, or take Cody with him. There had to be women at the rodeo willing to watch Cody while he competed. Wives, girlfriends and mothers of competitors regularly attended.

Mariana was going to come unglued. He'd promised her he wouldn't take Cody to a rodeo unless she came along. Also that he wouldn't make any decisions regarding Cody's care without her input.

It couldn't be helped. This was his last weekend to compete before Nationals.

Jacob did call Leeza and arranged for her to watch Buster. Then he threw together some of Cody's things for the trip. Did he have everything they'd need? Clothes, diapers, toys, snacks. If he forgot something, he'd simply buy it there. In between competing.

Thirty minutes outside of town, his cell phone rang. Jacob answered while simultaneously reaching into the backseat to pass Cody some animal crackers. Hopefully, that would stop the boy's constant crying.

"Sorry I missed your call earlier," Luke said.

"I figured you were busy."

"Sounds like you are, too."

After Jacob explained the situation, Luke offered to drive to the rodeo that evening. Jacob declined. By then, he planned to have a babysitter lined up.

"Are you sure?" Luke asked. "That's a lot of responsibility."

Did no one think him capable of caring for his son?

"I've got it handled."

"All right."

His lack of confidence irked Jacob.

Maybe he was biting off more than he could chew. A two-year-old at a rodeo with no advance child care lined up? That was taking a risk.

His goal, however, was just within reach. His do-or-die moment. No way in hell was he quitting now.

Mariana swung her Infiniti into the parking lot of their opposing counsel's law offices. She immediately spotted a familiar car belonging to one of her team members. The other three attorneys had driven to Houston together. Mariana requested to arrive separately so that she could leave early tomorrow and not have to wait on them.

Okay, she admitted it. She missed Cody and was a tiny bit worried about him. Not that Simone wasn't a great nanny.

She was also eager to be home before Jacob returned from the Valle del Sol Rodeo. Though that wouldn't be until Sunday evening, she wanted time to prepare a special dinner to celebrate his qualifying. One that included champagne, a decadent dessert, then something intimate, and a little naughty, for later, once Cody was asleep.

Sitting in her parked car, she placed another call to Simone, all the while chiding herself for being overprotective. Just because the nanny didn't answer was no reason to jump to conclusions. She and Cody might have gone outside to play. Or she could have put her phone on Vibrate because Cody was napping, and she didn't want anything to wake him.

When Simone didn't answer, Mariana left a message. Her call to Jacob also went straight to voice mail. He was probably traveling a remote part of the highway and out of range. Just as she was telling herself to relax, her phone went off in her hand. The relief she felt was short-lived. It was neither Simone nor Jacob on the line.

"Hello, Ray," she said.

The private investigator's deep baritone filled Mariana's ear. "Got some information for you. Finally."

Mariana automatically reached into her briefcase for a notepad and pen. "What is it?"

Adele Black had been good at covering her tracks. Ray's investigation into her background had hit a number of roadblocks, hence, the lengthy amount of time with nothing to report.

"She and Delia Baron are definitely one and the same person."

"You can prove it?"

"Have the documents and photos in front of me right now."

Ray was nothing if not thorough and dependable. He needed to be in his business, especially when the outcome of a court depended on his findings.

"That's good news." At least, Mariana hoped it was good news. Jacob's adoptive siblings may feel differently. "Send me a bill."

"This one's on the house. Without your help, we wouldn't have gotten half as much from that insurance company. My wife still brags on you."

"Anytime. You let me know."

"I'll email you the pics and docs the minute I hang up."

"Thanks. If I don't talk to you before, you and your family have a happy Thanksgiving."

"Same to you."

Mariana resisted calling Simone and Jacob again. If they weren't contacting her to report a problem, then she should assume all was well.

With only a few minutes to spare, she grabbed her briefcase and dashed inside the building. Her team members welcomed her with "You're late" and "We were starting to get concerned."

As it turned out, all the rushing and reprimands were for nothing. After being led to a large, tastefully appointed conference room, the team was made to wait. And wait. A young, professionally dressed woman, her features carefully schooled, came in to advise them the witnesses would be another ten minutes. Mariana figured it was a strategic ploy intended to unsettle them.

Mariana was unsettled all right. But only because she couldn't dismiss the niggling concerns that no amount of deep breaths assuaged.

"Excuse me a second," she said. "Be right back."

Ignoring the frowns of her fellow team members, she stepped outside the door, found a spot down the hall with a modicum of privacy, and made calls to Simone and Jacob. Still no answer. With a groan of frustration, she called Carly. Finally! A live person.

"How are you?"

"Fine." Mariana spoke in a low voice so that the employees passing by didn't overhear her. "My private investigator called. Brace yourself. He says Adele Black of AB Windpower is definitely your mother."

Carly audibly gasped.

"I'll email you the docs. I was only able to skim them, but they look legit."

"Oh, my God!"

They chatted briefly. Carly was concerned

about the reaction of her siblings. There would be relief, but also more questions. Why was AB Windpower, Adele Black, buying up Baron Energies' stock? There had to be an explanation.

Down the hall, the glass door to the conference room opened, and Trevor, the team's self-appointed leader, stuck his head out.

"I need go, Carly. I only have a minute, and I want to try the nanny again. For some reason I can't reach her."

"She's gone."

"Gone? What are you saying?" And how would Carly even know Simone's whereabouts?

"Jacob called a while ago. Your nanny's daughter was in a car wreck, and she had to leave."

"Oh, no!"

"From what he said, the girl's all right."

Mariana was glad for that, but her biggest concern was her nephew. "Where's Cody?"

"With Jacob."

She went weak with relief. "He stayed home."

Her next thought was that he'd miss the rodeo and his last chance to qualify for Nationals. Poor guy. He must be devastated.

"No, he didn't," Carly said. "He's on his way now to the Valle del Sol."

"He went to the rodeo? With Cody? Who's going to watch him while Jacob competes?"

"He said he'd find someone."

"Find someone!" A stranger would be responsible for her nephew.

Mariana's head spun. This couldn't be happening. Jacob had sworn he'd talk to her first before making a move regarding Cody's care. How long had that lasted? A week? Two?

He hadn't bothered telling her. Of course not; he knew she'd be mad. Maybe he really was in range and ignoring her calls.

"I'll talk to you later." Mariana didn't give her next move much thought. Zero thought, actually. She simply marched back down the hall to the conference room.

"I'm leaving," she told her fellow team members upon entering the conference room. "Family emergency."

"You can't walk out." Trevor gaped at her as if she'd lost her mind.

Quite possibly she had. Her potential promotion was on the line, if not her job. Mariana had poured her heart and soul into this case, as well as given countless hours. Throwing everything away at the last second was insanity.

She squared her shoulders. Saul would have to understand and not take her to task.

"I don't have a choice," she said. "You can manage without me."

The sound of her heels clicking on the floor didn't quite drown out the chorus of shocked outbursts.

It wasn't only Cody's well-being that motivated Mariana's hasty exit. It was the betrayal.

He'd as much as lied to her. And if he was going back on his word this early in their relationship, about something he knew was vitally important to her, what did that say about his character and his respect for her?

This, she thought angrily, was something her father would have done. Not take a toddler to a rodeo—he hadn't cared enough about Leah or Mariana to do that. But leave without telling her mother *and* purposefully doing something he knew she wouldn't like.

Mariana tried Jacob again. When the recorded message started to play, she hung up and tossed the phone onto the passenger seat. Next, she pulled over to the side of the road and programed the car's GPS. The Valle del Sol Rodeo was one hour away. She could make it in fifty minutes if she pushed.

Chapter 13

Mariana put work from her mind as she wove through the crowd at the rodeo grounds. Saul wasn't happy about her abrupt departure. In his opinion, Jacob's taking Cody to the rodeo didn't qualify as an emergency.

What did he know?

She also didn't think about the speeding ticket that very surly highway patrol officer had issued her. Eleven miles over the limit wasn't that much. And where did he get off saying it was fourteen? Mariana could fight the ticket. She *would* fight the ticket. Later. First, she needed to find Jacob and Cody.

Déjà vu. She'd been here before, done this

before. Not the Valle del Sol but another rodeo just like it. She was looking for Jacob then, too.

Seriously, Mariana. You are screwing up big-time.

The memory of Trevor's warning proved hard to ignore. He'd lectured her soundly during the drive, right on the heels of Saul's terse reprimand. Mariana paid less attention to Trevor, even though, according to him, the deposition wasn't progressing well.

You might as well kiss the promotion good-bye.

She hadn't liked the sound of that or the unmistakable glee in Trevor's voice. He was her biggest rival for the promotion. Saul had gone so far as to intimate Trevor might be the better candidate after all.

Did no one understand?

Jacob obviously didn't. Not about Cody or her. Earlier, she'd reached him. At last! He'd admitted to bringing Cody with him but only after Mariana mentioned her conversation with Carly. Had he intended to tell her at all or wait until she came home to an empty house on Saturday and freaked? Doubts assailed her, about him and about their relationship.

As a result, she didn't alert him of her plan to confront him, saying only that she wasn't needed for the deposition and had decided to join him at the rodeo. Perhaps because he was too occupied with competing, he hadn't questioned her.

Steer wrestling was his first event. Why he was competing baffled her. He wasn't close to qualifying. Only in bronc and bull riding. When she asked, he said he'd entered in order to get his head in the game.

Head in the game. Uh-huh. Rather than watching his son, he was competing in an unnecessary event.

Mariana quickened her pace. With each step, her anger intensified. She didn't stop to consider the cause or what she was going to say to Jacob once she tracked him down. Too much hurt clouded her thinking.

"Hey, lady! Watch it."

"Sorry." The guy wasn't the first person she'd jostled or bumped in her haste to reach the arena. Tugging her trench coat more closely around her, she continued on.

Maybe she should slow down just a bit. Concentrate. The bucking chutes and livestock pens weren't far ahead. Cutting behind the stands, she cast her eyes right, then left. Where was he?

Without slowing, she tried phoning him,

but the call went straight to voice mail. He must have shut off his cell. He did that when he was competing. She imagined his surprise when she strode up to him, fit to be tied. He could forget all about getting his head in the game then.

A high-pitched wail sliced through the noise of the rowdy crowd and straight into Mariana's heart. Cody? Could it be? She strained to hear. Yes. Definitely Cody. And he was in distress.

She made a sharp turn, almost trampling a small child. "Excuse me."

The child's parents scowled at her and snatched the boy away as if she were a danger to him. Did she look that angry?

Losing her bearings for just a moment, she found them again when Cody resumed his wailing. Was he hurt? Sick? Miserable? Being mistreated? In whose care exactly had Jacob left the poor boy? Her stomach twisted into a tight knot.

There! About twenty feet ahead. A young gal, she couldn't be more than sixteen or seventeen, held a flailing Cody in her arms. They stood on the far side of the bleachers, near the public restrooms. Clearly, the teen was incapable of handling Cody. Not getting whatever he wanted or needed, he was throwing the grand-mother of all tantrums that two-year-olds were famous for.

Another time, a different child, Mariana might have felt sorry for the girl and sympa-thized. Today, she just wanted Cody soothed and safe in her arms. Whatever the problem, she'd deal with it.

"Here, I'll take him," she announced, ap-proaching the gal. "He's my nephew."

The instant Cody saw her, he started squall-ing and kicking his feet every which way.

The gal came dangerously close to losing her grip. "What? Who are you?"

"Quick." Mariana opened her arms. "Before you drop him."

"Mama, Mama," Cody cried.

Mariana managed to grab hold of one foot. This young gal was obviously in way over her head.

"Go away!" The teen turned her body, put-ting herself between Cody and Mariana. "If you don't leave right now, I'll call security. I swear."

Cody's crying escalated.

"Perhaps you didn't hear me." Mariana forced herself to remain calm. "I'm his aunt."

"His father said nothing about any aunt showing up."

The gal might be young, but she was a little brighter than Mariana first gave her credit for. And, perhaps, a little more responsible, as she wasn't about to turn over Cody to a stranger. Not that Mariana cared. She wanted her nephew and nothing was going to stand in her way.

She employed her best attorney voice, the one she used to win over a client's confidence. "Would he call for me if he wasn't my nephew?"

"He wants his mother. You said you were his aunt."

Did Mariana resemble a kidnapper? In her suit and heels? She looked like something, apparently. Possibly a little crazed. People were staring as they passed. One of them might actually call security. She thought about showing her driver's license, but what would that prove? Her last name wasn't the same as Jacob's.

As much as Mariana wanted Cody, she'd rather not deal with a security guard or, worse, the police. "Let's call Jacob, okay?"

The gal's eyes narrowed to thin slits. "I'll do it." It required enormous effort, but she managed to extract her cell phone from her pocket while still holding on to Cody, whose face, by now, had turned beet-red.

"Are you all right?" A middle-aged man came over, his wife beside him. He wore a concerned expression. Hers was suspicious.

For one ridiculous moment, Mariana imagined defending herself in a court of law for trying to remove her nephew from the arms of his babysitter.

"There's been a mix-up," Mariana explained.

"No mix-up," the girl said over Cody's crying, her cell cradled in the crook of her neck. "His father was very specific. I wasn't to let him out of my sight for anything."

"Mama, Mama." Cody's flailing progressed to thrashing as he twisted to get a look at Mariana. The teen really was close to dropping him.

Mariana edged closer.

"No answer." The teen pocketed her phone.

"This is my nephew," Mariana insisted. "I was in Houston, taking a deposition. I'm an attorney." She looked at the couple, hoping her claim of belonging to a respectable profession would reassure them, if not intimidate them slightly. It didn't.

"If so, then why didn't the boy's father tell this young lady about you?" The man posed a good question, unfortunately.

"I wasn't able to reach him."

The man stepped closer to the teen. "Is there someone I can find for you?"

Even more people had gathered. This was getting out of hand.

Mariana made another attempt to reason with the gal. "I'm asking you to give me my nephew before something happens. Like he gets hurt."

That didn't go over well.

"Leave us alone," the girl shouted.

"What's going on here?" A deep male voice had every head swiveling.

Jacob emerged from the small crowd. His face was sweaty and covered in grime. His jacket hung open as if hastily donned, the dirt stains on his shirt visible. Apparently, he'd finished his steer wrestling run.

"Mariana?" He stared at her with confusion.

Without waiting for an answer, he went to the teen and took Cody from her.

Immediately, the boy stopped crying, shoved his thumb in his mouth and with his other arm, hugged Jacob's neck. Tears streaked his cheeks.

"Everything okay, Hannah?" he asked.

Mariana all but leaped on Jacob in her rush to comfort Cody. She assumed he'd immediately relinquish the boy. He didn't. "Jacob?"

"She said she's Cody's aunt," Hannah muttered, glaring at Mariana.

"She is."

"You didn't tell me about an aunt."

"I didn't know. I figured she'd wait for me."

Frustrated at not being able to hold Cody, Mariana crossed her arms. "I told you I was coming. Why didn't you let her know?"

All at once, the teen's composure broke down, and she sobbed, "Did I do something wrong?"

"Not at all. Everything's fine." Balancing Cody on his left hip, Jacob unzipped his jacket pocket, pulled out his wallet and extracted a pair of twenties. He handed them to Hannah. "Here. You can head back to your family now."

Her mouth fell open. "This is too much money. I only watched him a few hours."

The look Jacob sent Mariana spoke volumes. "I'm thinking you earned it."

"Thank you!" After relinquishing the diaper bag and giving Cody's head a pat, Hannah hurried off.

The crowd had also dissipated. Well, except for the middle-aged couple. "Everything okay?" the man asked Jacob.

"We're fine. Appreciate the help."

The couple left, but not before giving Mariana a cool once-over.

She was beginning to feel like a creep. Or worse. And it was totally undeserved. She'd done nothing wrong.

Jacob's angry expression said differently. "Quite a little show you put on."

She bristled. "I heard Cody crying. Screaming, actually."

"So you accosted poor Hannah?"

"I didn't accost her."

"Let's go." With his free hand, he latched on to her arm and walked her along beside him.

"Where?" she demanded.

"Someplace less public. I have an hour before my next event, and we need to talk."

"Good." Mariana shook her arm loose. "I couldn't agree more."

"Simone called right before you got here," Jacob said. "I forgot to tell you. Her daughter's fine. Home from the hospital. The car is a different story."

"I'm glad to hear that. About her daughter. Not the car." Mariana pressed her fingers to her temple as they walked. She was a little ashamed she hadn't given any thought to their nanny.

"She's sorry. Says she'll be back to work

on Monday. I told her not to worry and take all the time she needs."

"Sure. Fine. We'll manage."

Where were they going, for Pete's sake? The parking lot? Cody, still riding in Jacob's arms, kept up a nonstop stream of babble, pointing and waving.

"Relax, will you."

She stiffened at Jacob's admonishment even though it might be—okay, was—deserved. She had gone a little overboard.

"You didn't answer your phone," she said.

"And you terrified Hannah. She's just a kid."

"Now you admit it."

"She's an experienced babysitter, Mariana. Came highly recommended by several mothers here."

"She didn't look experienced from what I saw."

They were headed toward the practice rings. Jacob found a quiet area far away from the noise and commotion. The stack of straw bales provided a perfect seat—for Jacob and a drowsy Cody, who snuggled his face into the front of Jacob's shirt.

Mariana refused to sit. Not in her suit and not in her suede trench coat. She'd stand. Better yet, pace. This wasn't going to take long, after all. Jacob had mentioned competing in an hour. He probably wanted to be with his buddies, doing whatever it was they did before events.

"I'm not making a mountain out of a mole-hill," she insisted, anticipating his next remark.

His brows rose but he said nothing.

"You shouldn't have taken Cody without telling me."

"*Taken* him? I brought him with me. There's a difference."

The difference being Cody wasn't her child. "We agreed to make all decisions regarding his care jointly. And you're the one who insisted he and I not come to any rodeos after Lucky Draw."

"Okay. You're right on that count. Both counts," he amended after she started to object. "I didn't tell you because I knew you'd be upset. Which you are."

"That doesn't excuse your actions."

"Mariana, Cody isn't a bike or laptop we're sharing use of. There aren't rules of ownership. He's my son. I'm his parent."

And she wasn't.

Mariana raised her chin to hide her hurt. "That's right. I'm just his aunt. You get to call all the shots."

"We've been through this before. You're more than just his aunt."

"I was worried. About both of you. More than worried, I was scared. First, no one answered my calls. Then, when I get here, I see Cody with this girl. And he was throwing a fit. How did I know she wasn't abusing him?"

It was a stretch, she conceded that, but not entirely beyond the realm of possibilities.

"Put away your attorney hat for a few minutes. Do you honestly think I'd leave Cody in someone's care who wasn't competent?"

"You didn't know her before today." Mariana leaned a hand on the haystack for balance and removed one of her shoes. Making a face, she shook out a pebble, then replaced the shoe. "And you were letting this girl wander the rodeo grounds with him."

"Her name is Hannah."

"What if something had happened?"

"She had to use the restroom. Should I have told her no?"

"You could have watched Cody while she went."

"I was competing." He spoke slowly, as if she were dense.

Mariana took offense. "It always comes down to that. Rodeo, rodeo, rodeo."

"You're being way too hard on me."

A part of her agreed, though she wouldn't admit it to Jacob.

"I grew up with a father who put himself before everyone else. It eventually cost him the love and respect of his family. I don't want the same thing to happen to you. Cody needs his father."

"I left him with a competent babysitter. It's not as if I abandoned him."

"You did something you promised not to. My father was like that. Always taking my mother for granted."

"So this is about your father."

"You're a lot like him."

Now it was Jacob's turn to get angry. Deep lines appeared, bracketing his mouth. The hand not holding Cody clenched into a fist. Cody stirred, but fortunately didn't wake.

"You're a lot like your mother. Rigid and uncompromising."

"I am no such thing."

"It's your way or no way."

"That is not true!"

He shook his head. "We aren't arguing about Cody. Or Hannah and her babysitting skills. Or about my rodeoing, either. Your nose is out of joint because I made a decision without you."

"We had an agreement."

"It's one weekend."

"This time."

"Don't accuse me of something I haven't done. That's not fair."

All right. It wasn't. She made an attempt to restrain her temper.

He continued, his tone less contentious. "When we first decided that you would live with me, it was going to be temporary. You knew you'd be giving up the day-to-day involvement in his life."

"That changed." She swallowed. "At least, it did for me."

"It's changed for me, too."

"Then why lie to me about leaving?" She despised the desperation in her voice

"I've already admitted I was wrong. It won't happen again. What more do you want?"

"I've heard that before. From my father. When he was arguing with my mother."

If she'd wanted to wound Jacob, she succeeded. Pain and disappointment flared in his eyes. "Did this past week mean nothing to you?"

Remorse came, but slowly. "I'm sorry. That didn't come out right."

"I think it came out exactly the way you

intended." He stood then. Cody stretched, hugged Jacob tighter, then fell back asleep.

He adores his father.

It was as if a glass wall slammed down, separating Mariana from Jacob and Cody. They were father and son. She was on the outside, looking in. Oh, she'd always have a place in Cody's life. Jacob wouldn't shut her out entirely. But her involvement would be from a distance.

All along, she'd been afraid that Jacob would fall for her because their living arrangement was too cozy. Too easy. Too much like a normal family. In hindsight, she should have been concerned about herself. What if her feelings for Jacob weren't real? Merely a product of her fear of losing Cody?

She slumped against the stack of straw, no longer caring about damaging her suit or her suede coat.

Switching places, Jacob took up pacing.

"I'm not competing just because it's fun or a way to pass time. I'm doing this to secure a future for myself and my son. As a vice president of Baron Energies, I can give him the kind of life he deserves. The best upbringing. A decent education. A place in the Baron family that I fought for and earned. If he wants to follow in my footsteps, great. If not, also great. I'll support him regardless. He'll grow up strong and smart and able to make his own decisions."

It was quite a speech. Mariana felt his passion. His wishes for Cody weren't so different from hers. Other than, she didn't fit in there anywhere. Not once had Jacob mentioned her.

She tried reasoning with herself. Yes, his intentions were good. Admirable. Far loftier than her father's. But Jacob did what was good for him. His position in the Baron family and at Baron Energies. His son. His rodeoing.

Not her.

"Let me take Cody home," she said softly.

"Why?" He looked at her with uncertainty. Not deep and abiding affection as he had all this past week.

"You'll be able to compete for the rest of the weekend with no distractions."

"I'm not distracted. At least, I wasn't."

Another stab, intentional or not. She retaliated. "He'll be happier at home."

"He's happy here."

"Please, Jacob."

She hoped he didn't hear the desperation in her voice. Something told her if she didn't take Cody with her right now, she'd lose him forever. The fear was perhaps irrational and unfounded but also real and unsettling.

Jacob appeared to consider for a moment, then shook his head. "He's staying with me."

"Hannah can't possibly watch him all weekend."

"I have this handled, Mariana."

She'd taken her stand earlier. Jacob was taking his now.

"You're being stubborn for no reason," she said.

"I'm not the only one."

"You're also being selfish. You're denying me Cody because you're mad that I came here and made a scene."

"I'm not that petty."

"It makes sense for me to take him."

He didn't speak for a moment, giving Mariana hope that he'd come to his senses. It was quickly dashed.

"This argument of ours has nothing to do with Cody."

"No? What, then?"

"Your issues with your father. Guilt over your sister's death. You breaking your promise to her."

"You're way off base."

"When you're ready to level with me, then

we can talk. Really talk. Not use Cody as the rope in an unnecessary tug-of-war."

"If you won't let me take him home, I'm leaving anyway."

"That's your decision."

Her bluff had backfired. He was going to let her walk and do nothing to stop her. She'd been right. It was all about him. Him and Cody. He didn't care one whit about her.

Mariana could have cried, except she refused to in front of Jacob.

Her cell phone rang, giving her a start. She'd have liked to ignore it but the ringtone identified the caller as Saul. He'd have a fit if she didn't answer, and he was already mad enough at her. She pushed off the straw stack and onto her feet, then took a moment to compose herself.

"Hello, Saul." Mariana felt Jacob's eyes on her. *Boring* into her, to be precise.

"Trevor just called with an update on the deposition."

"And?" Had Saul changed his mind? Decided to be more understanding about her family emergency? She could use a little good news.

"Frankly, it's gone to hell in a handbasket."

"That bad?" She gnawed on her bottom lip.

"You're the expert on this case. The one who prepared all the briefs. We were counting on you to question the witnesses. Only you're not there. Molinas's attorneys were ready for us and blocked us at every turn."

"I'm sorry, Saul. Look, I can—"

"You can get back there right now. Trevor has somehow convinced opposing counsel to take a break until two. You have one chance to redeem yourself. If not—"

She cut him off this time. "You're going to take me out of running for the promotion."

"I'd better hear from Trevor in the next ninety minutes telling me that your bright, shiny face is sitting across from him, or I'm going to do more than take you out of the running. I'll fire your ass."

Mariana cleared her throat. "All right."

She ended the call, her fingers shaking as she re-pocketed her phone. It might have sounded as if she'd acquiesced to Saul's demand, but in truth, she hadn't fully decided.

Jacob must have heard Saul's end of the conversation or read the expression on her face, for he said, "You have to go. You've worked too hard on this case to give up now. Your clients are depending on you."

Work. He'd put that first because that was how Jacob thought.

It was how she thought, too. Didn't she? Up until lately, anyway. It hadn't seemed so important earlier when she walked out on the deposition. Her clients, however, did matter. She hadn't given her all to the case solely for the glory of the win or a promotion. She genuinely believed Molinas needed to pay for his crimes and that his victims deserved to be recompensed.

"Your advice is appreciated but not necessary." She tightened the belt on her coat.

"I'll call you later."

Would he? Probably. Did she want him to? That was another question.

"Goodbye." Mariana went over to Jacob, pressed a hand to Cody's back and kissed his cheek. "I love you, little guy. Be good."

His only response was a soft sigh. It closed like a noose around her heart.

Turning, she walked away, ignoring the pebbles that seemed to leap into her shoes.

"Mariana. Wait."

She kept moving, straight ahead, convinced she was leaving her entire universe behind but unable to stop. Jacob could come after her. Even carrying Cody, he'd catch up to her within seconds. Only he stayed put. What did that say about them and their relationship? Not anything she wanted to hear.

The walking out on the deposition, the scene with Hannah, the confrontation with Jacob, had all been for nothing. She'd let her fears get the best of her and cause her to make one bad decision after the other. She'd probably lost the promotion. Possibly lost her job. Definitely lost Jacob.

Mariana held back the tears until she reached her car. Not caring about the vehicle's underside, she sped out of the parking lot, gravel and dirt flying. At the main road, she aimed the car in the direction of Houston, the deposition and the slim chance of salvaging her career.

Tomorrow when she arrived home, a day ahead of Jacob, she'd pack all her belongings and move out. When he and Cody returned on Sunday, it would be to an empty house.

Chapter 14

Luck was on Jacob's side. He made it to the finals in all three bucking events—only by the skin of his teeth. Unless he totally screwed up, he was going to Vegas for the National Finals.

Every muscle in his body strained as he waited for his turn at bareback bronc riding. He'd drawn a good horse, one that should give him a heck of a ride. Saddle bronc and bull riding were iffy. This event, however, his first of the day, was in the bag.

He hadn't lied to Mariana. Cody was a champ all weekend. He slept through the night. Behaved for Hannah. No more tantrums.

It was Mariana who continually distracted

him. She crept into Jacob's thoughts every waking moment and into his dreams for the few hours a night he managed to catch some sleep.

He'd called her. Countless times. He lost track how many. Was she giving him a taste of what it had been like for her on Friday when no one answered her calls? Probably not. She simply didn't want to talk to him.

There had been a total of two text exchanges. In the first one, she let him know she'd made it to Houston and asked after Cody. The second one, yesterday, informed him that she was home. When he'd texted back asking how she was doing, she hadn't answered. Just like his calls.

He'd made her mad. Hurt her feelings. That was pretty clear. She'd made him mad, too, however. And, yeah, hurt his feelings. He'd done nothing these past weeks except to demonstrate his desire and willingness to be a good father. Yet she still didn't trust him.

Then why tell him about Cody in the first place? Why not keep him a secret as was her dying sister's wish?

Just one explanation made any sense. Mariana had assumed, before introducing him to Cody, that he'd be a deadbeat father like

Zeb Snow and not give a flying fig about his child. She'd have been able to keep her promise to her sister while still satisfying her lofty principles.

Killing two birds with one stone. A neat trick if true. Thinking it might be made Jacob madder. Had he been played all along?

Possibly. She'd certainly blinded him. Though it didn't really matter as the end results were the same.

"Hey, Baron," his pal and sometimes rival Keith called. "Aren't you listening? You're up soon."

"Be right there." Jacob struggled to clear the mental fog surrounding him. Just because he was closest to qualifying in bareback bronc riding was no excuse to lose focus.

Adjusting his chaps, he strode over to where Keith stood, balanced his forearms on the railing and studied the competition. This cowboy lasted 4.7 seconds, taking a mighty spill when the horse executed a death-defying spin.

Keith chatted about the next cowboy's chances as Jacob's horse was brought forward and positioned inside the chute. His eyes went automatically to the stands, but Mariana wasn't there.

Jacob ground his teeth together. Enough already.

"Mr. Baron."

At the sound of his name, Jacob glanced up to see a security guard approaching. Confusion set in. Why was the man looking for him?

"Yes."

"May I speak to you a moment?"

"Sure."

Keith cast Jacob a curious look as the short and beefy uniformed man joined them.

Had Mariana come back and given Hannah a hard time again? Instantly, he berated himself for thinking that. Perhaps his truck had been broken into. Or something had happened at home. His next thought was of Daniel. Then Brock. Then Lizzie and the baby.

"What's wrong?" he asked.

"First, let me say your son is all right."

"All right?" Jacob's gut clenched.

"There's been an accident. He fell from the bleachers. Your babysitter is with him at the first aid station."

"Is he hurt?"

"The EMT's examining him now."

EMT! Jacob didn't hesitate. "Which way?"

"Come with me."

"Jacob," Keith called. "Where you going?"

"I'll be back."

Would he? Not until he knew for certain Cody was okay.

He heard his son's wails long before they reached the first aid station near the rodeo office and experienced a little of the wild worry Mariana must have felt on Friday. Jacob covered the last twenty yards at a run, forgetting all about the security guard.

The boy sat on Hannah's lap while the EMT tried to affix a temporary brace on his arm. Cody would have none of it.

"Nooooo." He wrenched his arm free from the EMT's grip. "Want Mama."

Mama. Not Daddy. Only Jacob had sent Mariana away, more or less.

"Hey, buddy."

Cody swung his head around. At the sight of Jacob, his wails intensified, and he tried to crawl down Hannah's lap.

She hung on. "Mr. Baron. I'm sorry."

"Daddy, Daddy."

Jacob went over, and the babbling started as Cody tried to tell Jacob what had happened. The story was punctuated by hiccups and sobs. Jacob made out only a few words. Hurt. Arm. Migo. Mama again.

"Let me take him." Jacob and Hannah traded places. He sat in the metal folding chair with Cody while she stood beside them.

"I looked away for just a second, I swear." Hannah chewed on her stubby nails. "He didn't fall but three feet. Maybe four. I wouldn't take him that high up in the bleachers."

"It's all right, Hannah." Now that Jacob was holding Cody and assured that, while hurt, he was in one piece, his worry was abating. "I know from experience he can move pretty fast."

"You don't have to pay me," she insisted.

"Of course I'll pay you."

She broke down. Strangely, the sound of her crying quieted Cody. He stared at her with large damp eyes. That enabled the EMT to finish putting on the brace and apply an ice pack, which he secured with a long length of elastic bandage.

"Did he sprain his wrist?" Jacob asked.

"I'm pretty sure this little guy fractured his radial bone. Won't know for sure until his arm is x-rayed. And he's going to need some pain meds. That break has to hurt."

A break! Pain meds?

"But he's only two."

The EMT, a guy younger than Jacob, gave

him a look that said, "Hey, stupid, anyone can break a bone."

Hannah's mother appeared in the doorway, and Hannah ran to her. "Mom!"

"Sorry I didn't get here sooner," the woman said. "How is he?"

"A broken arm." Jacob still couldn't believe it. "Maybe."

"That's a shame." Her arm around Hannah had a calming effect on the teen.

"On the plus side," the EMT said, repacking his supply case, "children generally bounce back pretty quickly. Better than a lot of adults."

There was a plus side to a broken bone?

"I hate to be the bearer of bad news," Hannah's mother continued. "But your friend asked me to tell you that you missed your turn at bronc riding and were disqualified."

At the moment, that was the least of Jacob's concerns.

"He said you still have time to make the saddle bronc riding."

And the bull riding after that, thought Jacob. Only two chances left to compete. If he didn't, if he failed to qualify, there'd be no purchase of Starr Solar Systems and no new alternative energy division at Baron Energies.

He didn't stop to consider his choices.

Holding Cody to his chest, he stood. "Do me a favor, will you? Tell Keith I won't make it. I have to take my son to the emergency room."

Cody refused to let go of Jacob's neck as they walked to his truck. Hannah and her mother followed, bringing the stroller and diaper bag. While Jacob buckled Cody into his car seat, mindful of his injured arm, Hannah and her mother loaded the stroller in the back. A sippy cup of juice helped soothe Cody.

Hannah gave Cody a hug. "Sorry, little guy."

Hannah's mother offered directions to the nearest hospital.

"Thanks for your help," Jacob said, climbing into the cab.

"Good luck."

He was going to need it. Especially when Mariana found out.

Another rodeo, another injury. Only this time, it was his young helpless son. What kind of lousy father was he?

"See you tonight, Lucille," Jacob said. "Let me know if you need anything."

"I'll call when we arrive. And before we leave after supper."

He'd already loaded Cody into his grandmother's SUV, along with the diaper bag and an assortment of favorite toys, among them the stick pony. By trial and error, Jacob was learning what to pack extra of and what wasn't needed. Mariana had skipped that step in his daddy training.

He stood with his hand resting on the open driver's side door while Lucille buckled her seat belt and donned her sunglasses.

Their relationship had come a long way recently. Frustrated at being unable to reach Mariana after Cody's fall, he'd called Lucille instead. His reaching out to her seemed to have broken down the last of any barriers between them, for which he was glad.

"Leave a message if I don't answer," he said. "I might be at the drill site, and I don't always hear my phone." He'd traded mornings with Darius so that he could be here to see Cody off.

"Take care, Jacob."

"You, too."

He could only guess what Mariana had told her mother about their argument. Falling out. Breakup. Call it what you will. In Jacob's mind, it had been the former. Clearly, it was much more to Mariana. Relationships survived arguments. Theirs had disintegrated.

Lucille glanced behind her at Cody, who

kicked his feet and waved his casted arm in anticipation. She was taking him to visit Mariana, who had moved back to her duplex while Jacob was at the Valle del Sol Rodeo.

Without telling him. He still wasn't over that.

When Jacob and Cody had arrived home on Sunday evening after the rodeo, it was to an empty house. That had surprised him. Shocked him, as she hadn't known about Cody's broken arm.

Looking back, he should have anticipated something was amiss when she didn't text him asking when they were due home.

Once the shock wore off, her abrupt absence angered him. It took him a full day to acknowledge that his anger was an attempt to mask his pain. Her betrayal—there was nothing else to call it—had thrown him harder than any fall from a bull. He got that she was mad when she left the rodeo. But enough to move out? Enough to leave Cody behind?

Enough to leave him?

"Bye-bye, Daddy."

"I love you, pal."

Cody blew him a kiss from the backseat. That was new. He must have learned it at day care.

How many other firsts would Jacob miss when his son was with someone else?

More than he'd like, but there was nothing to be done about it. Jacob needed to work, and he certainly wouldn't deny Mariana and her mother visits.

"Tell Mariana hello for me."

"I will." Lucille smiled, though her eyes were sad.

The invisible vise that had squeezed Jacob's middle since he walked into his empty house tightened another notch. All communications with Mariana, all arrangements for this visit, had been conducted solely through her mother.

How had things fallen apart so quickly? One minute, Jacob and Mariana were a happy couple, crazy about each other and planning a future. The next minute, they were barely speaking. *Not* speaking. Had attraction and, as Mariana pointed out, the coziness of living together been the only things binding them? Apparently so, for the instant they hit a rough patch, they'd bailed on their relationship. Both of them.

Though Jacob had tried to talk to her. Repeatedly. But a man could only take so much rejection. He'd accepted responsibility for his contribution; namely, not telling Mariana that he was taking Cody to the rodeo. In his opinion, that was the extent of his wrongdoings. Mariana was the one who'd come unglued, uncorked and, if you asked Hannah, unhinged.

"Thank you, Jacob," Lucille said.

"For what?" He'd been expecting Mariana's mother to leave the instant she had Cody in her car. Yet here she sat, parked in his driveway.

"Letting me see Cody. You don't have to."

"You're his grandmother."

Tears sprang suddenly to her already-sad eyes. "I miss Leah so much. You never really got to know her."

"No, I didn't."

"She wasn't a terrible person. She just wanted a child more than anything."

Lucille was referring to Leah's tricking him into sleeping with her, then keeping her pregnancy and Cody a secret. "Of course she wasn't."

"You don't hate her?" Lucille stared up at him.

"I'm grateful to her. She gave me a son."

"I have to admit, you're a better father than I ever thought you'd be."

Her remark, so unexpected, touched him. "That means a lot to me."

"I did a terrible disservice to both my daughters. Hardened their hearts to all men because of my anger at their father."

Jacob kept quiet, unsure if she expected him to comment or not.

"She cares about you, Jacob. I haven't seen her fall for a man like she did you...ever, I suppose. It must have been difficult for her. Strange. Awkward. Being attracted to the man her sister seduced three years before."

He hadn't thought of it quite that way before.

"And with you being a rodeo man like Zeb." Lucille lost herself in her thoughts for a moment. "Mariana, she can be obstinate."

Wasn't that the pot calling the kettle black? Jacob almost laughed but didn't. Lucille had obviously been doing some soul-searching.

"I admire her. She fights for what she believes in. Personally and professionally."

"Telling you about Cody wasn't an easy decision for her. She was really torn between her promise to her sister and her sense of right and wrong."

"Both those qualities make her a good attorney." And someone Jacob admired.

"I can only guess that leaving you and Cody must have been equally difficult for her."

"Then why did she?" He answered his own question. "Because she couldn't face me."

Lucille drew back as if affronted. "She doesn't walk away. She sees her commitment through."

"Not this time."

"Losing her heart must have scared her. It scared me when I was young. Probably why I've always been uncompromising where Zeb is concerned. If I didn't work hard at hating him, I'd fall in love with him all over again."

That was the most revealing thing Jacob had learned about Mariana, and it came from her mother.

"Maybe you should tell her that," he said.

Something in Lucille's expression changed. "Maybe I should."

"Have a safe trip." He swung the SUV door shut, stepped back and waved to Cody.

She started the engine and drove away. Jacob didn't worry. Cody was in good hands.

With several hours to kill before having to head off to the drill site, Jacob ran a load of laundry and cleaned the kitchen. Outside, he filled Amigo's feed bin with hay and shoveled manure under Buster's watchful eye. He could afford to pay a part-time hand to oversee the horse's care but preferred to do it himself. Even on a chilly day like today, being outside invigorated him.

Normally, it invigorated him, he should say. Jacob hadn't felt himself since Mariana left.

He was just heading inside when his cell phone rang.

"Where have you been lately?" Carly demanded.

"Busy."

"It's not easy being a single dad."

"It's great being a single dad. There's just a lot involved."

"How's Cody doing?"

"Bouncing back." Exactly as the EMT had predicted.

"I'm really sorry about Mariana."

He didn't ask how Carly knew, assuming Mariana had told her. They'd spoken once or twice about Adele Black and AB Windpower. Many of the pieces were starting to come together. Jacob was glad for his adoptive siblings and glad Mariana had been able to help them.

"It is what it is." He hardly understood his feelings. How could he explain them to someone else?

"You miss her."

That did sum things up pretty good.

"She made her choice."

"If you ask me, she regrets it."

Could that be true? "I'm not running after her," he said.

"Why the hell not? She's worth it."

"Carly."

"Fine. I'll stop butting in." She drew a breath, then changed the subject. "Listen, you are coming to Thanksgiving dinner."

She said it as though he didn't have a choice, which he really didn't. Attendance at Baron holiday dinners was mandatory.

"For a while."

"What! You are not cutting out early, Jacob Baron."

Her tone was in jest. Jacob, however, wasn't finding anything humorous of late.

"Dad's asking about you," Carly went on, ignoring Jacob's lack of response.

"Tell him I'm fine."

"Come on, Jacob. You've been avoiding him."

With good reason, he thought. "I'm busy. Single parent. We talked about that. I'll see him tomorrow at Thanksgiving."

Where a houseful of people were available to buffer any interaction between him and Brock.

Jacob didn't want to look into the older

man's face. See the disappointment there. He'd left the Valle del Sol Rodeo before competing and failed to qualify for Nationals. Now there was no Starr Solar Systems purchase, no new position at Baron Energies and no Mariana in his life.

Jacob was batting a thousand.

"You're both being stubborn." His sister was still on the subject of Brock.

"What's he being stubborn about?" Jacob opened the refrigerator door, evaluated the contents, decided nothing appealed to him for lunch and shut the door.

"Talking to you," Carly said. "He thinks you should come to him. In fact, he's been sitting around the house since Sunday, hoping you'll make an appearance."

"You know what? He's right. We had a deal. I failed to keep up my end. I *should* go to him."

"It's not like that, Jacob."

"It's exactly like that."

"Then why won't you come to the Roughneck?"

"Tomorrow," he repeated.

She made a very unladylike sound of disgust.

"I've been thinking of looking for another job."

Carly gasped. "You haven't! Why?"

"I'm tired of waiting for Brock to promote me. If I can't have the kind of job I want with Baron Energies, maybe I should try somewhere else. There are plenty of companies that would hire me." On his last name alone.

"You'd work for the competition? Tell me that isn't true."

"I'd work for an alternative energy company. In fact, I heard from a friend that AB Windpower is hiring."

"Really?" That seemed to interest Carly.

"Yeah. Or one closer to Dallas." Jacob would consider changing jobs but probably not moving too far from Dallas. Mariana and her mother would miss Cody.

"Don't do it. Don't leave us without talking to Dad first. You owe him that much."

He did.

It was easy to blur the lines between business and professional. Wrong, but easy, and what had landed Jacob in this predicament in the first place.

"Thanks for not giving up on me," he told Carly.

That brought a smile to her voice. "See you soon."

Not long after ending his call, Jacob climbed

into his truck. His initial intention was to head to work early. Instead, he drove to the Roughneck.

He did need to talk to Brock. And what better time than the present?

Chapter 15

After stopping at the house and checking with Julieta, Jacob drove to the arena. Brock was right where she said he'd be, riding his favorite gelding. Luke stood at the fence, watching the other man closely.

"Should he be doing that?" Jacob asked.

Luke spun. Upon seeing Jacob, his face broke into a smile. "I was beginning to wonder about you."

Jacob fell in beside his friend. "I thought he was still mostly laid up."

"You know your dad. He insisted he was ready to ride. 'Course, I had to help him up on the horse. I'm not looking forward to helping him down."

"Nothing holds him back for long."

"Same could be said about you."

"That's kind of what I came here today to talk to him about."

"Good." Luke nodded approvingly.

Jacob started off toward the barn.

"Where you going?"

"I can talk just as good to Brock from the back of a horse as I can on the ground."

Luke's chuckle was loud and long.

Jacob made quick work of saddling and bridling Zeus. The big sorrel, always full of energy, nearly trampled Jacob in his haste to exit the stall.

The startled look on Brock's face when Jacob trotted into the arena was priceless. "Thought you were working today," he hollered.

By the time Jacob caught up with Brock, he was back to his usual grumpy self.

"Going in a little late. I called Darius while I was saddling up."

"The boss's being tardy doesn't set a good example for the employees."

"First time I've been late to work in over a year. I think I'm entitled."

Brock grumbled under his breath.

They rode in silence for several minutes, both horses wanting to step out, and both riders letting them. Jacob wasn't sure where to start. He settled on saying what was foremost on his mind.

"I know you're disappointed in me."

"Because you're late to work?"

"Not qualifying for Nationals."

"I won't deny it. I had my heart set on you bringing home a title."

"I think I could have, too."

"There's always next year."

Could he wait that long for a promotion? Jacob already knew the answer.

"I'm done rodeoing."

At that, Brock's bushy silver brows rose. "You are?"

"Cody is my number one priority."

"You'd have had help raising him if you didn't run that pretty little gal off."

"Mariana."

"I know her name."

"Did you refuse to say it just to make me mad?"

"Something like that."

There might have been a touch of amusement in Brock's voice. It was hard to tell.

"She was more to me than just help raising my son."

"Maybe you should have told her that."

"I did."

"Did you show her?"

Was Jacob's entire family going to lecture him about Mariana?

"I would if she'd take my damn calls."

Brock burst out laughing.

"That wasn't a joke."

"Which makes it all the more funny." The older man sobered. "When your mother and I married, it was mostly for convenience. She wanted to give her boys a new life, a new name. And I need someone to run my house, mother my children and attend social functions. I suspect you know that."

"I guessed."

"I cared for her, though. Greatly. She was a fine woman with a good heart and gentle soul. And while our feelings for each other might not have been the stuff poets write about, I let her know every day, one way or another, that she was important to me. That I appreciated all she did for me and my children. That I valued her as more than just a partner or an accessory at business dinners."

He had? Jacob didn't remember. Then

again, maybe the ways Brock showed his affection and appreciation were small and personal. He hadn't ever thought of Brock as the sentimental or romantic type.

"She cared for you, too."

"I'm thinking what you feel for Mariana—" he emphasized her name "—is more the kind of love poets write about and much too valuable to lose."

"Fatherly advice?"

"I am your father." Brock brought his horse to a stop. When Jacob did, too, Brock looked him square in the face. "I'd be more of one to you if you let me."

Let him be a father? When had Brock ever let Jacob be his son?

"I think you have that wrong."

The brows rose again. "Do I? You've shut me out from the beginning. At first, I understood. You were nine. Not ready to accept a new father, regardless of how angry you were at Oscar for what he did to you and your mother. So I gave you your space. Only you didn't change. No matter how hard I tried, you shut me out."

He'd tried? Jacob examined some of his memories with a different perspective. Was it possible the distance he'd felt from the Barons had been his own doing and not Brock's? The closeness he'd recently established with Carly and Lizzie seemed to suggest as much.

"I came here today to tell you I'm going to look for another job." His admission took him by surprise.

Not, apparently, Brock. He didn't so much as blink. "Is that really what you want?"

"No. I want what I always have. To run an alternative energy division at Baron Energies. And someday, maybe my son will follow in my footsteps."

"That'd be nice. You did follow in my footsteps, and I didn't have to drag you kicking and screaming like Jet."

Frustration had Jacob jerking too hard on the reins. He forced himself to loosen his grip.

Hadn't he worked hard enough? Proved himself? And yet Jet was going to run Baron Energies one day alongside Lizzie while Jacob remained senior safety manager. If he was even still working for Baron Energies.

"I did everything you asked of me. The only reason I didn't qualify for Nationals is because my son fell and broke his arm. I took him to the hospital. Which was more important. And if I had to do it all over again, I wouldn't change a damn thing."

The corners of Brock's mouth lifted in a grin. "You'd better not. Or you're no son of mine."

Jacob glared at him. "I don't understand you sometimes."

Again, Brock didn't so much as blink and smoothly changed the subject. "If you hadn't avoided me since Sunday you'd know the purchase of Starr Solar Systems was final yesterday. They're expecting you in their offices on Monday."

"What! Are you serious?"

"As a heart attack." Brock nudged his horse into a walk.

Jacob went after him, still trying to wrap his brain around the past two minutes.

"What made you change your mind?" he asked when he caught up.

Brock reined to a stop. He looked surprised. "Nothing."

"But I didn't qualify. That was the deal."

"The deal was you prove yourself. You did that." He leaned forward and stacked his forearms on the saddle horn. "I might've been good about telling your mother how I felt, but it seems I've been lacking where you're concerned. I'm mighty proud of you, Jacob. You've done right by your son and the family name. It took real courage to walk away from that rodeo when you believed you were leaving everything you'd worked for these past years behind. I respect that in a man."

Jacob shook his head in amazement. "You're a stubborn old coot."

"Takes one to know one."

Hadn't Carly said the same thing?

At the barn, it was Jacob and not Luke who helped Brock down from his horse. When they were both on the ground, they shook hands.

"Thank you," Jacob said, a slight huskiness to his voice. "I won't disappoint you."

"I'm counting on it."

He did something then he couldn't remember doing since his high school graduation. He hugged Brock.

"Get your ass to work," his father told him. "You're going to need to spend some time with Darius, getting him up to speed to replace you."

"He's a good choice for the job."

Brock just grumbled again.

Luke also shook Jacob's hand when he shared his news about Starr Solar Systems. "You going to tell your sisters?"

"Later. I'm running late."

It wasn't them he wanted to tell, or Daniel. All Jacob could think about as he unsaddled and brushed his horse was Mariana. If things hadn't gone wrong, she'd be the one he called first. The one he celebrated with tonight over the best dinner in town.

Was his family right? Should he go after her?

Without giving himself time to change his mind, he pulled out his cell phone and dialed her number. Five rings later, her voice mail message played.

Nothing had changed. She still wasn't taking his calls. His elation sank like a lead balloon. Instead of leaving a message, he hung up.

Mariana sat at her desk, rereading the email from Jacob's sisters for the third time. While it came from Carly's account, all three names appeared at the bottom: Carly, Lizzie and Savannah.

They were being sweet. They'd thanked Mariana profusely for her help with locating their mother. Still figuring out their next step, they'd yet to make contact with Adele Black. That would come, however, they'd assured her. They also invited Mariana to Thanksgiving dinner at the Roughneck.

You're family, the email had said.

In a roundabout way, Mariana supposed she was. Aunt to the oldest Baron grandchild. Had things gone differently with Jacob, she might have been related in another, closer, way.

Speaking of Jacob, the email continued with, Our brother is a jerk with the intelligence of a gnat.

Their support was also sweet. But Jacob hadn't been the only one demonstrating a lack of intelligence. Their argument at the Valle del Sol Rodeo, and her behavior since, wasn't exactly her most shining moment.

The most startling part of the email came near the end. Wasn't sure if you heard, Jacob has quit rodeoing and was promoted to VP of Alternate Energy.

No, she hadn't heard, and Mariana was admittedly curious about what had changed Brock's mind. Jacob hadn't finaled for Nationals, the condition placed on him. Instead, he'd walked away. Unbelievable.

Not for most guys. She'd expect most fathers to put their son first, hurry him to the hospital after a fall. But Jacob? He'd wanted that promotion more than anything. More than her.

When she'd first heard about Cody's accident, her concern had been solely for her nephew. After learning the break was only a hairline fracture and would easily heal in a matter of weeks, her relief turned to anger. If Jacob had just let her take Cody home as she wanted to, none of this would have happened.

The anger phase didn't last and was replaced by sorrow. She should be there. With Cody. With Jacob. Who wasn't rodeoing anymore.

What if she'd waited and not been in such a damn hurry to move out of his house? What if she hadn't made a scene at the rodeo? They might have survived this rough patch. Instead, she'd been—what were the words Jacob had used? Oh, yeah. *Rigid and uncompromising.* In other words, a control freak.

Great for an attorney. Not so great for a romantic partner. Or a parent. With an attitude like that, Cody would grow up to hate her. All right. *Hate* was too strong. But he wouldn't love her to pieces.

Mariana had so much to learn. Fortunately, she still had a chance with Cody. But Jacob? She feared that ship had already sailed. Problem was, it might not have if she'd answered even one of his phone calls.

Staring at the email from Carly, she debated how to phrase her reply. The obvious response to their dinner invitation was to say she was visiting her mother and grandmother for the day. Jacob's sisters would accept that excuse without question.

Except Mariana hadn't exactly said yes to her mother's request. Something kept holding her back.

She knew she should go. It wasn't, however, what she wanted. The visit wouldn't include Cody, who, by prearranged agreement, was spending the holiday with Jacob.

Two weeks ago, Mariana had imagined her mother and grandmother driving up from Austin, and all of them going to dinner at the Roughneck. It could have been special. Memorable. Their first Thanksgiving as a family. Now she was staying at home, alone and licking her wounds.

"You're here!" Saul had popped his head through the door of Mariana's tiny and cramped office at Hasbrough and Colletti. "Thought you might have left by now."

"Soon." She minimized the open window on her computer, hiding the email from Jacob's sisters. "Just finishing up a few things."

Three o'clock on Thanksgiving Eve, and

most of the employees were long gone. Mariana hadn't noticed anyone walking the halls for the past ten minutes. Then again, she'd been lost in thought.

"I'm glad," he said. "Saves me tracking you down."

"What's going on?"

Saul stepped into her office and lowered himself into the one visitor chair. The knees of his long legs bumped her desk. He swore under his breath.

"We're going to have to do something about this."

Mariana gestured to the piles of folders and documents, surrounding her like a castle wall. "I don't think I can manage with a smaller desk."

"What about a larger one?"

"Funny."

"To go with your larger office."

"A girl can dream," she said offhandedly, part of her glad for the interruption, part of her longing for solitude.

"It's no dream."

At the strange note in his voice, she looked up.

"Congratulations, Mariana."

"Congrat—" Her jaw dropped. "Are you…? Does this mean…?"

"The partners met after lunch."

"But I…" She was still struggling to make her mouth work properly. "Paulo Molinas. The case is—"

"Going to be closed on Monday. His attorneys forwarded another settlement offer this morning." Saul handed her a file.

She took it, not realizing until that second he'd been cradling several files in his arm.

Her pulse picked up speed as she quickly scanned the papers. "This is good."

"Are you kidding? It's freakin' fantastic. Our clients will be thrilled."

"I'm glad." She let out a shaky breath. Her terrible Thanksgiving had just improved a tiny bit.

"I thought, as our newest junior partner, you'd like to place the calls."

"I walked out of the depositions. I don't deserve this."

"That did tick me off. I won't lie. But you went back and kicked some serious butt. Found the holes in their arguments and blew them wide-open. They were nervous after that and with good reason. You deserve the promotion, Mariana."

She'd done it. Obtained a decent settlement

for her clients *and* landed the promotion. It meant...

...not as much as it once had. Oh, she was happy. And her family would be pleased and excited for her. But calling her mother with the good news wasn't the same as hurrying home to share it with the one you love.

Yes, she loved Jacob. If only she hadn't let a passel of other emotions obscure the one that truly mattered.

"Thank you," she said softly and laid the folder on her desk. "I'll start making the calls now."

"You'll need a new case to keep you busy." Saul handed her another folder. "One befitting a junior partner."

Mariana leafed through the contents of the file, her initial excitement waning. The daughter of a state representative had possibly, might have, maybe-not-so-accidentally walked out with sensitive information from the securities firm where she'd interned over the summer.

"Thanks, Saul." Mariana released a sigh. "You do know this isn't the type of client I want to represent."

"But it's the type of client who comes to us. The type who pays our salaries and the ones you're going to have to represent as a junior partner."

Perhaps she should rethink her goals.

He smiled and handed her the third and last folder. "Which is why I'm giving you this case, too. Mr. Colletti thinks it'll be good for the firm's image."

From the Heart, a small nonprofit support group for widows and widowers whose spouses had died from catastrophic heart attacks, had been forced to vacate their offices due to a questionable, and potentially unethical, clause in their lease agreement.

For the first time in days, Mariana felt the heaviness that was her constant companion lift. "Thank you, Saul."

"It's pro bono, of course," he said.

"Of course."

"We need people like you at Hasbrough and Colletti. For balance."

"I'll get started on both cases right away. After I make these calls."

He rose. "Don't stay late."

"Sure, sure." She was already making notes.

At her door, he paused. "For the record, burying yourself in your job isn't a solution."

Her head snapped up. "I'm sorry?"

"You're not the first person who's used work to escape grief, Mariana."

Pain caused her throat to close. She needed a few seconds to recover before answering. "It was just a relationship, Saul. I'll be over him soon."

"I was talking about your sister." His smile turned melancholy. "My dad died last year. It's only recently I went from thinking about him every hour to only once a day. Give yourself a chance to heal, okay?"

Mariana wasn't sure how long she sat there after her boss left. Five minutes? Ten?

Eventually, she pulled herself together and called her mother.

"Have you decided about tomorrow?"

"That's not why I called, Mom. Saul just left my office. I got the promotion."

"Oh, honey! That's wonderful."

"It is."

"You don't sound happy."

"I'm thrilled."

"Call him."

"Who?" Silly question. Mariana knew exactly who her mother was referring to.

"He really cares about you. I can tell."

"Mom."

"Don't live your life like me, always asking

yourself the same questions over and over. And they always start with 'what if.'"

"I need to go." Mariana couldn't continue the conversation. It was simply too painful. "Love you, Mom. Call you tomorrow."

She barely hung up in time before the tears started falling. For Leah, for Cody, for Jacob and for the utter mess she'd made of her life.

Chapter 16

The Baron house had been taken over by an army. There wasn't an empty chair to be found. Jacob stood off to the side of the great room, counting heads and then eventually giving up after thirty-six.

Their family was growing by leaps and bounds. In the past few months alone, they'd added Lizzie's husband, Chris, and their baby; Savannah's fiancé, Travis; Carly's fiancé, Luke, and his daughter, Rosie; Jet's fiancée, Jasmine, and her twin girls; and, last but not least, Cody, who refused to wear his sling. At the moment, he was stuck to Julieta's son, Alex, like a second shadow.

Thank goodness the boy liked Cody and was willing to play with him. That didn't stop Jacob from keeping a watchful eye on the pair of them. If they were anything like him and Daniel at that age, getting into trouble was simply a matter of time.

Friends were also here today, some of them business associates, others more like extended family. Only Mariana and her mother were missing.

They'd been invited by his sisters and by Jacob. Mariana had politely refused. On the plus side, she'd taken his phone call last evening. Their conversation had been cordial, though stilted, and about as friendly as talking to an IRS agent.

Jacob didn't let himself think about whether or not he wanted her back. That would be self-torture, seeing as she'd made it clear she was done with him. The best he could hope for was an amicable relationship for Cody's sake. Regardless of her refusal to come to dinner, Jacob was determined that Cody see his aunt and grandmother every holiday and birthday and as often as possible. In fact, if they got sick of seeing Jacob's face, that was fine by him.

Luke sauntered over. "If you'd smile a little more your sisters wouldn't fret so much about you."

"Did they send you check on me?"

"What do you think?"

"That interfering is a habit they'll never break."

"They care about you, Jacob."

"It's mutual."

The realization settled over him, warm as a winter coat. Sometime recently, the invisible barrier between him and the rest of the Barons had thinned, then evaporated. He still wasn't quite as close to his adoptive siblings as he was to Daniel, but they were making strides. The thought made him happy and took the worst of the edge off missing Mariana.

"Actually," Luke said, "there's something I want to talk to you about. If you have a minute. Your sisters gave me an excuse."

"What's up?"

He nodded toward the patio door. "Can we go outside? I don't want to humiliate myself in front of everybody."

This was sounding interesting. Jacob recruited Savannah to keep tabs on Cody, then said to Luke, "Lead the way."

The weather had cooperated for the holiday. It was cold but sunny. The two men kicked back on the wicker patio chairs, each with a beer in his hand. Jacob relaxed, an arm stretched across the back of the chair. Luke, on the other hand, fidgeted.

"What's got you tied in knots?" Jacob asked the question in jest. To his surprise, Luke wiped perspiration from his brow.

"There's sure an awful lot to this getting married stuff," he said.

"Are you having second thoughts?"

"God, no! Carly's amazing. I couldn't have found a better woman."

"Then what?" His friend's behavior was so out of character, Jacob had to stop himself from laughing.

"I was thinking, wondering if maybe you'd be willing to…" Luke drew a breath. "I'd be honored if you'd serve as my best man."

Jacob waited before responding, afraid his voice might betray him. "The honor is mine. Of course I will."

Luke grinned and wiped his brow again. "It's kind of involved. Tuxes. Rehearsals. Carly has these ideas about exactly the kind of wedding she wants. You might regret your decision."

"Never."

"Thanks."

Jacob did laugh then. "Don't know why you were so nervous."

"Like I said, there's an awful lot to this wedding stuff. But man, it's going to be great once we're married."

Jacob listened quietly as Luke outlined some of his and Carly's plans. Try as he might, he could only think about him and Mariana. They might have been the ones picking out new furniture. Buying a vehicle suitable for a growing family. Looking at preschools. Combining households and joining bank accounts.

"I could have lost her, you know."

Jacob mentally roused himself. He should have been paying better attention. "I doubt that would have happened."

"Naw, it's true. Luckily, I came to my senses and swallowed my pride." Luke stared intently at him.

"Do I sense a lecture coming?"

"I'm not the lecturing kind. But there might be a lesson in there I'm trying to convey," he conceded unabashedly.

"I must have called Mariana fifty times."

"Did you go see her?"

"Wha—? No."

"Pride." Luke leaned back in the chair and

folded his arms over his middle. "A damned inconvenience."

"You're wrong."

"It's easier to hide behind a phone call than face someone in person."

Jacob would have objected, except his friend was right. His efforts, though many, were token at best.

"She's told me time and again that I'm not the kind of man she's looking for. Nothing I've said or done has changed her mind."

"You are that guy, Jacob. Look at you. Great dad. Great job. Great future ahead of you. Except that part where you screwed up and let Mariana go. Could that be what she's talking about?"

"What am I supposed to do? Knock on her door and say, 'Hey, sorry about that fight we had. Thought you should know, I did it. Baron Energies' newest VP. Now you don't have to worry about me rodeoing.'"

Luke shrugged. "Do you love her?"

"Hell, yes."

"Then what are you still doing here? It's Thanksgiving. You should be with her."

Jacob had carefully planned every step of his life since high school. Junior rodeo. College. Working for Baron Energies. Returning to rodeo in order to win a title and Brock's approval. Then one day, Mariana had appeared in his life, telling him he was father to a little boy. Nothing was the same since.

And he wanted that craziness back.

He stood, nearly knocking the wicker chair over in his haste. "I have to go."

Luke also stood. "I'll tell the family."

In the kitchen, Jacob apologized to Julieta. "I have a favor to ask."

She readily agreed. "Anything."

Looking around at all the food, he asked, "Can I take some leftovers with me?"

He supposed, since dinner had yet to be served, the food wasn't technically leftovers. Julieta didn't split hairs and quickly assembled enough food for six people, packing the plastic containers into a paper bag.

Jacob grabbed Cody on the way out, nearly forgetting the diaper bag.

Brock appeared before they reached the door, blocking their way. "Where are you going?" he demanded.

"To beg Mariana's forgiveness and ask her to take me back. I'm bribing her with food and Cody."

"Well, don't just stand there." Brock clapped him on the back. "Daylight's wasting."

"Bye-bye, Gampa." Cody gave Brock his trademark squeezing fingers wave.

Brock grinned and ruffled Cody's hair. "Is it too soon to get him a pony?"

"Let me work on Mariana. First things first."

Because he carried precious cargo, Jacob obeyed the speed limits, though it was hard not to put pedal to the metal. Traffic, however, was light. He didn't panic until he reached her duplex. The place had the quiet look of no one home.

"Mama?" Cody asked, peering out the window.

"Yeah, Mama's house."

They stood at Mariana's front door. Jacob carried the bulk of the food. Cody had been given responsibility for one container, and clutched the mashed potatoes to his chest. After the second time ringing the doorbell, Jacob's spirits sank. She must have gone to Austin after all.

Suddenly, the latch clicked, and the door opened.

"Hi, hi!" Cody jumped up and down in place, then, dropping the potatoes, flung himself at Mariana, hugging her leg.

She lifted him into her arms and squeezed

the living daylights out of him. "What are you doing here?"

Jacob took her in from head to toe, refusing to hurry. It had been much too long since he'd last seen her.

"You look great," he said.

With her free hand, she tugged on the hem of her sweatshirt. "I've just been hanging around the house all day."

"You should do it more often." He liked her power suit and designer jeans. He liked the sweats, too, knowing firsthand the sexy curves hidden beneath the baggy material.

"Kiss," Cody demanded. Without waiting, he gave Mariana a loud smacking peck on her cheek.

Jacob briefly wondered if the same technique would work for him. Rather than take a chance at being rejected, he retrieved the container of potatoes and held up the paper bag.

"We brought food."

"I…ah…"

"Invite us in, Mariana."

Surprise must have given him the advantage, because after a moment's hesitation, she stepped back and allowed them entry. Jacob had been here twice to move Cody's things. He'd forgotten what a charming place she had. Small but comfortable and nicely decorated. Would she consider moving?

He made straight for the kitchen. Setting the bag of food on the counter, he removed his jacket.

"Why, Jacob? The visit. The food." She lowered Cody to the floor. He instantly ran off down the hall, probably to his old room. "Cody, come back."

"Let him be for a minute." Jacob began unloading the food. "Are you hungry?"

"Why are you here?" she repeated.

"It's Thanksgiving, Mariana. A day people traditionally spend with their families."

"You should be with yours."

He turned to face her. "I am. You and Cody are my family."

"Jacob." Tears glistened in her eyes.

"I've been really stupid."

"No, you haven't." She wiped her cheeks with the back of her hand. "A little stubborn, maybe. We both have."

"Same thing."

She laughed then, but it had a sad quality to it.

"I want to fix this. *We need* to fix this, Mariana."

"The food, bringing Cody, I really do appreciate it. But it's hardly enough to resolve our problems. A lot of damage has been done."

She was right. More drastic measures were needed. "I love you."

"Oh!"

Crossing the short distance separating them, he stopped in front of her and clasped her upper arms in his. "I think you love me, too."

"Jacob—"

"Say it," he insisted.

"I love you, too," she whispered.

"Thank God." He pulled her to him and tucked her head to his chest. "I was trying so hard to do the right thing by Cody, I did the wrong thing by us."

"You had a lot of help from me." She sniffed.

"Are you crying again?"

He drew back in order to gaze into her eyes. Eyes he thought he could get lost in for the rest of their lives.

"Maybe a little."

"Can we start over? Date like regular people? Move in together eventually because it's what we both want and not because it's convenient for Cody?"

"A date? Dinner-and-a-movie kind of date?"

"One without Cody. Simone can watch

him. I'll have a lot more time now that I'm working regular hours, Monday to Friday, eight to five, and not rodeoing."

"I might have trouble getting time off. Saul gave me two new cases." Those eyes he could get lost in lit up. "Molinas's attorneys settled. I made junior partner."

"Congratulations!" He lifted her into his arms and swung her in a circle.

"Jacob!" she squealed.

He set her down. "Hasbrough and Colletti made the right choice."

"I wasn't sure at first. Now, I am."

"Is that a smug smile you're wearing?"

"Could be."

"We'll work around your schedule. Just promise me we'll have at least one night a week together, even if it's just sitting at home in sweats watching TV."

"You make it sound easy. Like we can just start fresh."

"We can."

"I've made a lot of mistakes, like bolting at the first sign of trouble."

"You did do that."

"I'm serious."

"I am, too."

She laid her palms flat on his shirtfront.

"We can't afford to make mistakes. Not with Cody's care and well-being at stake."

"Everybody messes up. It's part of parenting. Our kids will survive."

"Kids?"

"I was thinking of two or three more."

"What!" She backed away. "Getting ahead of ourselves, aren't we?"

He grinned and reached for her. "Maybe a little. I'm willing to wait. Say, a year."

"A year! More like three."

"Two. We'll compromise."

"You are—"

She didn't get to finish her thought. Jacob cut her off with a kiss. When they broke apart, she was flushed, breathless and at a loss for words. Good. He liked her discombobulated.

"Do you know what tomorrow is?" he asked.

"The day after Thanksgiving?"

"It's also Black Friday. The busiest shopping day of the year. You free?"

"For shopping?"

"Ring shopping. I want to marry you, Mariana. Say yes," he told her when she started to protest.

"Yes!" Cody hollered. He came skidding around the corner and collided into Jacob and

Mariana. "Yes, yes, yes!" Holding on to each of their legs, he grinned up at them.

"There," Jacob said. "It's settled."

Mariana looked affronted. "He can't answer for me."

"I think he just did."

She gazed up at Jacob, love shining in her eyes, and tenderly cupped his cheek with her hand. "I was wrong, you know. You aren't anything like my father."

"I'm going to make you happy."

"You already have."

"I'll take that as an official yes." Jacob kissed her again, his fully healed heart beating soundly.

"Hug, hug." Cody pulled on Jacob's shirt.

"Good idea, buddy." Jacob bent and scooped Cody up.

With his son in one arm and Mariana in the other, he held his entire world.

A man couldn't ask for a better Thanksgiving, a better life, than this one.

* * * * *

Get 4 FREE REWARDS!

We'll send you 2 FREE Books plus 2 FREE Mystery Gifts.

Both the **Harlequin® Special Edition** and **Harlequin® Heartwarming™** series feature compelling novels filled with stories of love and strength where the bonds of friendship, family and community unite.

YES! Please send me 2 FREE novels from the Harlequin Special Edition or Harlequin Heartwarming series and my 2 FREE gifts (gifts are worth about $10 retail). After receiving them, if I don't wish to receive any more books, I can return the shipping statement marked "cancel." If I don't cancel, I will receive 6 brand-new Harlequin Special Edition books every month and be billed just $4.99 each in the U.S or $5.74 each in Canada, a savings of at least 17% off the cover price or 4 brand-new Harlequin Heartwarming Larger-Print books every month and be billed just $5.74 each in the U.S. or $6.24 each in Canada, a savings of at least 21% off the cover price. It's quite a bargain! Shipping and handling is just 50¢ per book in the U.S. and $1.25 per book in Canada.* I understand that accepting the 2 free books and gifts places me under no obligation to buy anything. I can always return a shipment and cancel at any time. The free books and gifts are mine to keep no matter what I decide.

Choose one: ☐ **Harlequin Special Edition** ☐ **Harlequin Heartwarming**
(235/335 HDN GNMP)   **Larger-Print**
(161/361 HDN GNPZ)

Name (please print)

Address   Apt. #

City   State/Province   Zip/Postal Code

Email: Please check this box ☐ if you would like to receive newsletters and promotional emails from Harlequin Enterprises ULC and its affiliates. You can unsubscribe anytime.

Mail to the **Harlequin Reader Service**:
IN U.S.A.: P.O. Box 1341, Buffalo, NY 14240-8531
IN CANADA: P.O. Box 603, Fort Erie, Ontario L2A 5X3

Want to try 2 free books from another series? Call 1-800-873-8635 or visit www.ReaderService.com.

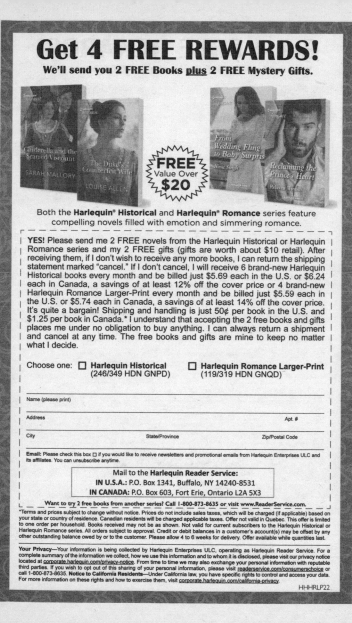

Get 4 FREE REWARDS!

We'll send you 2 FREE Books plus 2 FREE Mystery Gifts.

FREE Value Over **$20**

Both the **Romance** and **Suspense** collections feature compelling novels written by many of today's bestselling authors.

Visit ReaderService.com Today!

As a valued member of the Harlequin Reader Service, you'll find these benefits and more at ReaderService.com:

- Try 2 free books from any series
- Access risk-free special offers
- View your account history & manage payments
- Browse the latest Bonus Bucks catalog

Don't miss out!

If you want to stay up-to-date on the latest at the Harlequin Reader Service and enjoy more content, make sure you've signed up for our monthly News & Notes email newsletter. Sign up online at ReaderService.com or by calling Customer Service at 1-800-873-8635.